WHISPERS IN THE WIRING

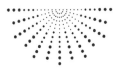

AMANDA APTHORPE

For Alison

CHAPTER ONE

Rupert reached into the top of the wardrobe. His hands groped among the many books and the few items of clothing. When he felt the rough texture of the cloth, he knew he'd found his mark. His fingers traced the hard edges of its contents. Lifting it down he placed it on the bed, smoothing the quilt around it. He sat carefully on the bed's edge and loosened the cloth to reveal a solid black plastic box and sat back from it, staring at it in quiet disbelief, the fingers of his left hand twisting the plain gold ring on his right. Rupert picked the box up again and held it to him, unable to comprehend that the brother he loved so much was now reduced to an area smaller than a lunch box. He had expected something more fitting for his brother's remains, but the weak voice of practicality reminded him that he lived in an age of disposability. The absurdity of it struck him and might have brought a smile to his lips were it not for a weight that was dragging at his heart. He wished that he could unburden that weight. He felt it physically, a heavy sensation in his chest that drew strength from his arms and legs and caused his breath to come in sharp gasps and to leave in long, fractured sighs.

He turned the box around until the plastic stopper was facing him — the stone across his brother's tomb. His thoughts drifted in a black and grey kaleidoscope and came to rest on the last conversation he'd had with Ross. He remembered the pain in his brother's voice, unsuccessfully disguised by too much alcohol, and the chilling sound of his despondency when he sighed and said that he didn't think he was of use to anyone anymore.

"But you mean something to *me*! And to Neti!" Rupert had replied with urgency but also a small amount of irritation. He *had* listened as he always had. He *had* told Ross what he meant to him. He just wished that he'd never put down the phone; that he'd *kept* talking to him. If only he'd known that they would never speak again.

But how could he have known? How many times had those conversations taken place? That instance, like so many others that had occurred all through their lives, caused Rupert to wonder where personality originated. It couldn't lie in the genes as some scientists claimed — Ross was his identical twin. If it were in the genes then Rupert too, with the help of a whisky bottle, would have tried to obliterate the pain of living and rammed his car into a tree. Or, conversely, Ross also would have chosen the safety of religious life and lost himself in the rituals and self-admonishments in an attempt to suppress the ego.

Rupert picked and prized at the plastic stopper that popped open to reveal the contents inside. No angels at the tomb, he thought ruefully. He held the box up closer to his eyes and could just make out the greyness of the ash against the black interior. His hand and the box dropped to his lap.

"Oh ... Ross ..."

The weight was dragging at his heart and constricting his throat, preventing him from breathing. The feeling was made worse by his attempt to stifle the sobs that were straining to be released. His mind raced through an assortment of images of his life with his twin — childhood scenes confused with adult conversations, the face of his brother one minute laughing, the next sobbing into Rupert's chest.

Gathering himself together, he sat upright. He lifted the box again and, tilting it towards him, dipped two fingers tentatively through the opening. The ash felt cool and some adhered easily to the sweat on his fingertips. He withdrew them and stared at them blankly, his mind having shifted to that empty space known to those in shock. Closing his eyes, he lowered his head to his chest and brought the fingers to his head. Lightly touching the space between his eyebrows, he began to apply the ashen traces of his brother to his forehead in a barely discernible sign of the cross.

Remember Man That Thou Art Dust.

CHAPTER TWO

Had only two weeks passed since Marjorie would find Rupert in the staff room spending time between lectures in easy chatter with colleagues? Now, after his brother's death, he more often slipped quietly into his office and, she imagined, shut the door behind him in relief.

Marjorie knew this was where to find him. She knocked and entered his study at his invitation. He was sitting marking papers by the window. In the ten years that Rupert had inhabited this office, very little had changed. He was an orderly man, sometimes to a fault. As a teacher though, he was renowned for his knowledge and his patience. Marjorie fancied that she could tell more about her staff on visiting their offices than she could by visiting their homes, which for some, like Rupert, was just a room in the College. For most who taught theology here, teaching was their life, and their offices reflected that life. Sometimes they were sad places, especially for the residents, no photographs of family and friends, no impractical presents from children, no sign of other interests or hobbies. However, this was not true of

Rupert, and in some ways, this was his contradiction. His office was sparse, but there were photographs, small ones in wooden frames of his mother, his brother Ross, and of his niece, Neti. These did not sit publicly upon his desk, but on the bookshelf across the room. Each photograph, she noted, was angled to take in the others while also facing him at his desk.

He looked up and smiled at her; she was struck by the gauntness of his face — not that anyone else seemed to have noticed, or if they had, no one had commented. Perhaps it was the light diffused by the old diamond-paned windows behind him that made his skin look sallow and his eyes appear haunted. She wished he would turn on the light so that she could appraise him more carefully.

"Hello," he said.

She stood inside the doorway. There was something about this time of the afternoon that made her feel melancholy, as if life itself might decide whether to continue or not. In the clearer light of the earlier day, everything seemed to have more reality. This College, its yellow sandstone buildings and carefully maintained gardens, successfully gave the impression of all that is solid and established, of order and substance. But in this light, this twilight, the sandstone wall that Marjorie could now see through Rupert's window was colourless. The students milling at its base looked tired and less self-assured than they had only a few hours earlier. She looked at Rupert, who was making a final correction to the paper in front of him, and, for a moment, Marjorie was struck with a sense of futility, as if all that took place within the College walls — the supposed sense of purpose and commitment — amounted to nothing.

I must be tired, she thought.

Rupert rose from his seat, gesturing towards the two chairs on the far side of the room.

AMANDA APTHORPE

He crossed the room and waited for her to sit before seating himself opposite her.

Marjorie placed the envelope she was carrying on the coffee table between them. She looked into his eyes.

They're haunted, she thought.

His normally long, thin face was thinner still and pale, almost grey. Marjorie feared for him. Rupert was forty-two and, although he was lean and conservative in his habits, he was of an age at which two of their colleagues had suffered sudden heart-attacks; one of them fatally.

"How are you? ... We miss you in the staff room."

"I'm all right."

She leaned towards him, her voice dropping a tone.

"How did it go at the weekend?"

There was a pause before he answered.

"Well, we scattered his ashes where he wanted."

His voice was practical and steady, but she noticed the colour rise in his face.

"That's about it really ... It's all over now."

"What about Neti?"

He cocked an eyebrow.

"She made an inappropriate comment at an important moment."

Marjorie noticed the flicker of irritation on Rupert's face.

"It's probably the only way she knew how to cope with it."

"Yes."

"How are the two of you getting along?"

"Like any fifteen-year-old and a stuffy forty-year-old might!"

"Your words or hers?" Marjorie said smiling.

A small smile forced itself onto Rupert's lips.

"Mine. Neti would never use a tame word like 'stuffy'."

"When are you moving?"

"Neti's away with her friend's family at the moment. I'll move into the house tonight. She'll be home tomorrow."

Marjorie took an intake of air and let it out slowly as she spoke, "It's not going to be easy ... You've lived here for a long time on your own."

"I know, but I lived in the religious community for twelve years," he offered with hope. He looked down at his hands. "I'm going to need your advice on raising a child — an adolescent, I mean."

Her eyes followed his to the gold band on his finger.

"Ross's ring?"

He didn't look up.

She spoke to his bent head, "Will everything be all right Ru, financially, I mean?"

Thoughtfully, Rupert raised his head.

"Despite Ross's limitations as a father, he has left a considerable legacy for Neti. It makes me wonder if he knew ..."

The air felt heavy between them. She reached for the envelope on the table.

"I thought you might be interested in this."

She slid the letter from its jacket and held it out to him.

He took it from her. "What is it?"

"A letter ... a request from a post-graduate student — PhD, I think, in neuroscience. She is wanting to interview anyone here who has had 'an intense religious experience' to use her words. I thought you might—"

"Oh no ... no ... I don't think so," he said handing the letter back to her.

"Just think about it."

She slipped the letter back into the envelope and placed it on the table as she rose to leave.

He rose with her.

Marjorie paused at the door and placed her hand on Rupert's arm in a gesture that revealed their long friendship.

"It might be what you need ..." she said, "to talk about it again."

He saw her expression and smiled. "I'll think about it."

Rupert closed the door behind her and turned back to his desk, avoiding the envelope still sitting on the table. The marking of papers seemed to be an endless task, made more so by the fact that he had to reread sections of students' work more often than usual. He found it difficult to focus on the content, and when he did, it seemed to be trivial and irrelevant. He knew that this was unfair, that each student deserved his full attention and to be taken seriously. Since Ross' death and funeral, however, it was increasingly difficult to assign significance to anything. When Ross was alive, he hadn't thought that his brother gave his life its motivation, but it now felt that there was little reason to go on without him, except for his responsibility to Neti. He didn't want to end his life, but he felt that if it did end, it wouldn't matter. If Ross could go ... so could he. He remembered that he had even felt some envy as the coffin was lowered to the flames. He didn't want to be the one left behind and felt that the greatest void existed in living, not in dying.

He thought about Neti and how she felt. She had given nothing away emotionally in the last two weeks. At her father's funeral, she sat impassively, studying her nails, although her chin was tucked close to her chest as if to contain anything that might leak from her heart and mind. He felt overwhelmed by the need to protect her but was daunted by the responsibility he was about to take on.

At his brother's home, that was now to be his own, Rupert poked at the charred logs he'd placed too early on the fire, hoping that something would take. He wanted the house to be warm and cheerful for Neti's arrival home, but he seemed to be thwarted in his attempts. He wondered whether he should put on some music, or perhaps the television, to create an atmosphere that might alleviate the inevitable silences between them. He decided on the television, which was now creating an uncomfortably chirpy background and made him feel like a court jester waiting in the wings to perform to a temperamental monarch.

He didn't know what Neti liked to eat, except for the various types of junk food he'd seen her consume with gusto on outings with Ross. A stock-take of the pantry revealed his brother's absence sharply. Rupert pictured him selecting each item from the supermarket shelf. In the end, the pantry's contents gave him no assistance; it seemed that father and daughter had lived on three-minute noodles and sauces found in jars with nonsensical names. He resorted to ordering Chinese take-away; he'd found a phone number, along with those of many other home-delivery restaurants under colourful magnets on the refrigerator. Even the simple task of ordering for them both caused him some anxiety. He was becoming acutely aware of his worldly incompetence.

Stepping into his brother's home had been difficult. He had not been here since the day Ross had died in the accident. Neti had been away on school camp and was due back that day; he suspected that her absence for a week unleashed Ross's fatal drinking spell. Rupert had waited at the school for the buses to return from camp. She was not surprised to see her uncle instead of her father — Rupert occasionally had to fill in when Ross was away on business trips. He remembered that she was flushed with excitement about the trip and full of stories about friendships made and lost; he also remembered, too vividly, her face when he told her about her father — how she turned a ghostly white and sat back from him, suspicious of his motives in telling her something like that. She had kept that distance ever since.

On this day, he would attempt to recreate a home for her. Concerned parents of Neti's friend had asked to take her in immediately until living arrangements were sorted out and so little had been disturbed at the house. When Rupert came in, the door to Ross's bedroom was closed. Inside, the room was tidy and the bed made. Ross's slippers were lying just inside the door and were askew, as if someone had thrown them in quickly and shut the door. Rupert had stared at them, too easily picturing them on his brother's feet. He slipped off his own shoes and stepped into them. His breath caught in his throat, and he quickly took them off again and shut the door behind him.

One hopeful flame burst from the embers in search of loose, dry bark. Rupert stood, flexing his body to ease the strain on his lower back. He turned around and scanned the lounge room, trying to imagine he was looking at it through Neti's eyes. Lamps on, television on, fire almost glowing, flowers in the vase on the coffee table. Is this what it would have looked like when she came home from school to her father? Too often she would have found Ross in a state of depression, with alcohol on his breath when she kissed him hello. No doubt Ross had tried to hide it from her. He was a good and loving father, but the eyes and ears of a fifteen-year-old are acutely tuned to the fraudulence of adults.

. . .

Leaving the residential college at the university where he had lived for ten years had been much harder than Rupert had thought. When he'd arrived, he'd been an eager thirty-two. He was more than ready, after twelve years in the seminary, to share his knowledge and his faith with his students — and he was satisfied with his calling. Occasionally over the following years, he'd fantasized about living in what some people called the 'real world' — marriage, children, mortgage; he wondered if he was missing out on something. Very often though, these were fleeting fantasies. His role as priest, and more particularly as confessor, exposed him more than most to the darkness of the human heart and, although he felt a genuine compassion, he could not empathize. Nor did he want to. Instead, he found himself wanting to distance himself further from the everyday human experience. That marriage and family life were not for him was reinforced by Ross's bitterly unhappy marriage and separation, but it had its roots much earlier in his own unhappy childhood.

When he'd closed the door to his room for the last time the previous day, he knew he was also closing a significant chapter of his life. To the outside world, his life would not appear to be much different; he would continue lecturing and carrying out his duties as the College chaplain. But his internal life was undergoing changes, the nature of which he could not determine, nor did he want to — he sensed that danger might be lurking there.

Rupert turned back to the fire, his eyes flicking along an assortment of photographs on the mantelpiece. From the corner of his eye, one of them caused him to start. It was a picture of Neti and Ross, but he had thought for a moment it was himself. Although they were identical twins, neither could really understand the difficulty others, even their own parents, occasionally had in telling them apart. Looking now at this photo, he was taken aback. What would Neti think when she walked into her home and saw him? A surge of panic went through him. She had always known him, seen father and uncle together, and she had faced him during the terrible weeks of Ross's death, but tonight was different. He was to be her guardian, living with her as her father had, and this was the beginning of that life together.

He heard a car door close in the driveway and the car leave. What was he to do? Open the door to greet her wearing Ross's face? Should he be doing something? Maybe with his back to her, humming nonchalantly, so that when she said hello, he would turn his head slowly, allowing her to adjust to the sight of him? Before he could decide, she was opening the front door. He bent down to the fire and stabbed at it repeatedly with the poker and began to whistle a cheerful tune. He heard the door close loudly behind her, announcing her arrival in a clear statement. His stomach lurched and the set of his jaw would no longer allow him to whistle.

Neti seemed to be unaware of him standing by the fire when she walked through the lounge-room from the front door. Although she must have known he would be there, she didn't seem to be looking for him. Instead, she headed resolutely to the kitchen, her gaze fixed ahead, the stiff movements of her body betraying her tension and giving her a slightly uncoordinated gait.

"Hello," he said from behind her. He noticed that her hair was now a combination of bright red and brown streaks that had been cut into short, aggressive spikes.

"Welcome home."

She froze mid-stride and seemed to be debating whether to

keep going. She turned her head slowly, the rest of her body still facing its preferred direction.

"Hello."

She said it without raising her eyes to him. The first of many silences fell between them, filled only by the drone of the television. He was glad now that he'd put it on.

Rupert thanked Polly's father who was waiting at the door and noted his look of sympathetic concern as he handed Rupert Neti's bags of clothing.

"If there's any way that I can help ..."

Rupert thanked him, sincerely wishing that he could.

When he returned to the lounge room, Neti was in the kitchen.

"You haven't eaten, have you?" he asked too cheerfully. He continued quickly, trying to stifle the silence that answered him. "I've bought some Chinese food."

"I'm not hungry." Her eyes lifted to his. There it is, he thought, the look of panic and pain. But it was fleeting and was instantly replaced with a look of contempt.

He had imagined that, on her return home, she would run to him as she had as a little girl. He had pictured her crying into his chest as he consoled her. Instead, she faced him coldly, half a room separating them.

"I'm going to bed."

She turned on her heels, steered away from the kitchen and headed up the passage to her bedroom, slamming the door behind her.

———

Almost as soon as it left her hand, Neti regretted the force she had applied to the door. She threw her bag into the corner of the room and fell face down on the bed, burying her head into the pillow. She flipped onto her back and lay staring at the ceiling looking for the old familiar patterns in the cornices; the tiny imperfections that were like secret messages from a master craftsman of an older time. Normally she found comfort in the shapes and chips that took on the appearance of animals and faces of imaginary people who had been her childhood friends, but tonight she couldn't empty her mind enough to allow them to manifest.

She rolled onto her side to look at the streetlights through the window, but nothing engaged her there. She rolled to her other side and let her eyes wander over the bits and pieces on her bedside table. She studied her collection of small china horses; rock pieces she had collected with her father on Sunday drives, each piece clearly defined by the light of the lamp that her uncle had put on earlier to greet her home. Standing out sharply from these was a small red bird made of cloth, stitched with gold and coloured thread, a Luck Bird her mother had sent to her many years ago after one of her many trips to Thailand. That's what her father had said anyway, with a note of sarcasm in his voice. She must have sent it not long after she left them, but Neti had not received anything more in ten years. She often wondered if her father had intercepted the gifts and had, a couple of times, looked in his room for unopened parcels and letters addressed to her. She had never found anything but was certain that they must exist. A mother would not just forget about her child — she was sure of that.

Neti propped herself up and took the bird from the table. She ran a thumb gently over its surface, circling its large woven eyes over and over. She could not remember much about her mother, but her father had given her a few photographs of happier times when they were a family. Still holding the bird, she opened the drawer of the table and took out a black book with an inset lock. She rummaged through the graffitied pencil case on the floor and produced a tiny key. From the back of her diary, she took out a photograph. It was of herself as a newborn resting in the crook of her mother's arm, her father sitting beside them. She dwelled momentarily on his image before placing her thumb over his face and, concentrating on that of the woman staring back at her, looked for similarities in her mother's face to her own. She decided that, yes, she could recognise some common traits; here, in the downturn of the eyes, there, in the soft cleft of the chin.

What had happened between her parents? She had asked her father, but he became subdued and would only say that her mother found it hard to adjust. Adjust to what? Neti felt that he had waited for his wife to return, and so she too lived with that thought. She placed the bird on top of the photograph, its body obscuring her father's face. Her mother would come home, she thought. She must come home now.

Still standing with his back to the smoking embers, Rupert winced as the door slammed. There was a moment of *déjà* vu — of walls shuddering as doors slammed and of malignant silences that grew between his feuding parents.

A long-buried but familiar knot was forming in his stomach. He automatically assumed the deep-breathing method he had devised in his childhood as a coping strategy.

What was he to do about Neti? His uncertainty rooted him to the hearth. Rupert forced his feet to cross the room to the passage and to her door. He raised one hand, knuckles bent for the knock, but drew it away again before making contact. He leaned forward, resting his forehead on the cool wood while he debated his next move. He thought he could hear her sob in an otherwise silent room. He straightened himself and raised his hand again only to see the lamplight go out from under the door.

He turned back to the lounge room, switched off the television, turned the armchair to the face the fire and sank into it.

For a long time, Rupert sat staring ahead, his mind in such a confusion of thoughts that, if asked, he would have said that he had no thoughts at all. He hadn't slept well for the week leading up to this day and after a few hours fell into a light sleep. His body twitched as his mind sank through the levels of sleep. At its deepest point, his breath came evenly but his eyes darted behind his closed lids.

Ross is here sitting beside him, a glass of whisky in one hand, cigarette in the other. Rupert is happy to see him but is not surprised. They have often sat here together. There is one difference this time — Ross is dead. His presence, though, is confirmation that life after death exists and Rupert is relieved.

"What is it like?" he asks with anticipation, only vaguely surprised that Ross is still drinking.

"It's all right ... Nothing in particular."

And there is that all too familiar desolation in Ross's voice. He swills his glass and takes a sip, the clink of the ice echoing through Rupert's growing emptiness.

His misery, heightened by the chill of the room, woke him. He opened his eyes and stared blankly ahead while his brain tried to reconcile the objects in his brother's home with the expected sight of his old bedroom. He felt drugged from a sleep that had brought him no relief. He placed the screen in front of the fire, switched off the lamp and retired to the small guest's room at the rear of the house.

CHAPTER THREE

The sound of the telephone ringing jarred the silence of the office and caused Rupert's pulse to quicken. He had become suspicious of the motives of the telephone and the sound of a knock on the door — they could only bring bad news. He wondered if he would always be like this. What had once been innocuous enough sounds seemed now to be loaded with ill-meaning.

Reluctantly, he picked up the receiver, "Hello."

"Hello." The woman's voice at the other end of the telephone sounded cheery, and not the bearer of bad news. He relaxed a little.

"This is Rupert Brown."

The caller introduced herself as Athena Nevis.

There was a pause that suggested to Rupert that he should know who she was. She must have heard his hesitation as she continued quickly.

"I'm researching my PhD at this university, and you volunteered to be a subject?"

'Volunteered' sounded more energetic than Rupert's

memory of his response. 'Coerced', by Marjorie, would have been the truth.

He had not expected this to be so soon. He was uncomfortable with the whole idea of discussing an event in his life he felt had little significance now. However, he knew from his own experience how difficult doctoral research could be and how necessary it was to legitimize theories.

Rupert invited her to his office the following Tuesday, and they exchanged pleasant farewells. He wrote the appointment into his diary. Athena Nevis sounded older than most of the PhD students he had supervised. Her name, however, suggested that she was from a generation younger than his own.

He wondered what use his own experience could be to her. From what he understood, she was looking for a biochemical factor in experiences of heightened perception, such as in moments of spiritual revelation. He had had one of these many years before. It had been an immensely significant event to him once — the catalyst for his conversion to Catholicism and taking religious vows. Now, he felt anxious at the thought of it, even embarrassed.

He busied himself, shuffling papers at his desk trying to forget about it. He went to the window and looked across to the oval where an end-of-season cricket match was being played in the early autumn light. He needed a distraction, he thought, and left the office to join the spectators, though he sat apart from them. The sun warmed his back and made him drowsy. Through heavy eyelids he watched the players go about their game. The woody sound of bat on ball and the calls of the players lulled him into sleep. He leaned back on the grass and closed his eyes. He slept more peacefully than he had in a while.

Marjorie saw him from her office. She had caught sight of him as he wandered down to the oval. She watched him now as he sank slowly back into the grass and thought she could imagine him groaning as he did so.

There had been a complaint from a student. Normally, this would not concern her unduly. Her position as Dean of the Faculty meant that she often had to deal with clashes of personalities between students and staff members, although never before concerning Rupert. But this complaint was more disturbing. Rupert, according to the student, made statements during his lectures that were counter to Christian doctrine. Sometimes, a particularly conservative student might find some of the more liberal views of scholars difficult to bear. However, Rupert was calling into question the Resurrection — not in terms of the interpretation of that fundamental event, but he had said that he doubted that it could have happened at all. Though Jesus of Nazareth was a great man, he had said, his life would have ended with his crucifixion, and it was quite likely that the disciples were deluded in their grief. The problem was not so much that Rupert thought this, as Marjorie too had wondered at times about the reality of the Resurrection. It was that he had voiced it in his teaching.

Marjorie left her office to join him on the grass. She sat quietly beside her friend, watching the steady rise and fall of his breath, a measure of the depth of his sleep. She studied Rupert's face. It was a face that she trusted and one that she loved. They had come to this University at the same time, both in their early thirties, full of enthusiasm and secure in their faith. They had each lived in the same college for years, until her marriage to John. They had shared their thoughts, argued out their different approaches to Christianity — he from the Catholic Church and she from the Uniting Church. She knew about his conversion from the Anglican tradition, and she knew about the profound experience that had triggered it. Rupert had told her one evening as they walked back to the College after dinner. She remembered how deeply the experience that had occurred many years before had affected him. She had always been moved by the intensity of Rupert's faith, the complete and utter commitment to his religious life, and he had been influential in her own decision to become an ordained Minister.

And now ... here he was — a tired body and a withering soul. She sniffed.

Rupert opened his eyes slowly at first and then wider in surprise.

"Are you getting a cold?" he said tenderly.

"Must be," she said, rummaging through her pocket for a handkerchief. She held it tightly to her nose.

"Ru ..."

"Yes." He sat up on his elbows.

"There's been a complaint Ru, from one of your third-year students."

"Oh, the Resurrection?" He looked away from her towards the match that was still being played.

She told him what the student had said, addressing his profile. Finally, he turned to face her.

"What do you want me to do?" he said without emotion.

"Are you admitting that you *did* say it?"

Although she suspected that the student's story was true, Marjorie was hoping that Rupert would deny it strongly.

"I probably did."

Marjorie felt a wave of exasperation.

"Ru ... *Why?* You know you can't ... You have a responsibili-ty." She was agitated, but more out of concern for Rupert than for the actual incident. She could probably smooth over that one.

Rupert placed his hand over hers.

"I'm sorry Marjorie. You're right of course. I don't know what made me say it."

"I'm worried about you Ru. You're not yourself. It's understandable under the circumstances, but ..."

"It won't happen again. I'll be careful in what I say."

Although Marjorie might have been relieved with this response, she wasn't.

"But it won't be what you believe, will it?"

He looked away from her again, still holding her hand.

"I don't know."

Marjorie let out a sigh of resignation at what she should do for him. She slipped her hand out from under his.

"I want you to take some of your leave, Ru."

He looked at her, perplexed.

Hardly bearing to look at him she continued quickly, "I think you need it. You need to settle into the house and to allow time for the adjustments that both you and Neti need to make."

"How long?" Rupert said, with some resignation.

"Four weeks. That will cover the coming school holidays anyway. Perhaps you and Neti could go away?"

Despite the strain showing in Rupert's eyes, there was a glint of humour in them at Marjorie's last remark.

"That would be fun," he said.

With a smile, Marjorie reached for her friend's hand and clasped it tightly in hers.

"Settled?"

"Settled," he said.

Subject 1
Name: *(Dr) Rupert Brown (SJ)*

Age: 42
Sex: *Male*
Occupation: *University Lecturer in Theology*
Medical History: *Sinusitis, occasional migraine, no chronic illness; no history of mental illness.*
Family: *to be provided in person*
Family Medical History: *to be provided in person*
Please outline below the nature of your experience of heightened perception: *to be provided in person*

Athena held the file in her hand as she ascended the staircase to Rupert Brown's office. He had provided little information that she could use, but he had bothered to return the form. She had wondered if he was going to be prickly to interview, but their brief telephone conversation had been pleasant enough and he sounded quite accommodating.

She scanned the closed doors in the corridor for his name and found it on one that stood slightly open. She knocked and the door opened.

Athena held out her hand to the tall, lean man who extended his in greeting.

"Hello ... I hope I'm not too early?"

She was carrying a red coat and he offered to take it from her to hang on the rack inside the door.

Saying little else but a warm hello, Rupert directed Athena to the chairs.

"Thank you for responding to my letter," she said as she sat down.

"I thought it was important that we meet in person first," he said.

Athena thought of the response he had written on the form and nodded in agreement.

She sat at the edge of her seat. The man sitting opposite her intimidated her and she was not sure why. She wondered if it was because he was a priest. Although he had not stated this on the form he had returned, she was aware of the significance of 'SJ' included at the end of his name. Only now as they sat facing each other did she dare to take him in. Yes, he looks forty-two she thought — pallid complexion, sandy hair carefully combed, a long nose which made his eyes look beadier than they might have against a smaller one. There was a softness to those eyes though; there was a heaviness around them made him appear tired.

As much as she was able to, Athena took in the office around her. It seemed an appropriate one for a theologian, although slightly cliched; wood-panelled walls, bookshelves filled, she assumed, with heavily weighted words, diamond-paned windows that let in a mellow light and a large oak desk. And yet, it was a simple office too and surprisingly void of religious symbols, except for a small cross on the wall behind him.

"Well," he said smiling, bringing his hands together in a prayer-like position.

She had to contain a smile when she saw that but began to relax.

"Can I ask why you responded to my letter?"

Rupert shifted in his seat.

"I'm not sure, but I was persuaded by my boss."

His voice was gently articulate with a timbre that was soothing yet commanding. It would be easy to listen to his lectures, Athena decided. She had wondered about Rupert's 'boss' as he described her and had been surprised that the dean of Theology was a woman.

Rupert answered her query.

"The College is ecumenical and it's not that unusual these days for women to hold such positions ... except in the Catholic Church of course. Tell me about your field."

"Well, it's neuroscience, as you know. What can I tell you?"

"Everything probably. I know very little about it. How did you get into it?"

Already becoming lulled by that voice, Athena reassessed it and decided that his was the voice of a priest, someone to whom it might be easy to confess. She considered her work in answer to his question.

"I sort of fell into it. No ... Fell in love with it. I did my Honours degree in biochemistry and somewhere along the way I became intrigued with the idea that our chemical composition might be underestimated ... that our bodies are at the mercy, to a certain degree, of our internal chemical soup."

He seemed puzzled, so she continued.

"Thoughts, emotions ... the works!"

Rupert was silent for a moment while he considered what she was saying.

"So ... religious experience, do you mean?"

Buoyed by the opportunity to talk about her work, Athena answered quickly, "A result of particular combinations of neurotransmitters flowing across synaptic junctions, exciting the next neuron."

"Like an epileptic fit." he said, but it sounded more a statement than a question.

Athena could feel herself blushing and wished that she'd spoken less hastily.

"Well ... look I don't know enough yet. That's why I'm researching."

"How many have responded?"

"You're the first."

They both smiled. She continued.

"But there has been some work done overseas."

"And what do you think might trigger one of these fits? Too many Brussel sprouts?" he said with a laugh.

Athena could feel herself growing redder.

"I didn't call it a fit ... And I don't know, that's why I'm researching. To find the trigger".

"A pity you don't have access to the brains of some of the saints. You'd find some hefty cocktails in those neurons."

He was smiling, but Athena could not determine if he was making a fool of her. She paused before replying.

"From what I've read, some of their experiences seem to have been symptomatic of manic conditions."

"Yes," he said, "I think that's probably right. Our mental demons manifest in strange disguises — addictions, suicide, crime ... religious experience."

"I didn't mean ..."

She saw him look away; noticed the slow blink of the eyes. There was a sense that he was implying something, about himself and his own experience. She answered, more gently now.

"I don't know what it is or why."

"But you think the experiences are not transcendent," he said, looking at her directly.

Aware that there was more to this question than he was revealing but uncertain what answer he was looking for, Athena could only answer honestly.

"I *believe* that there is a physiological explanation."

"I'm sure you're right."

There was no hesitation in his reply, and, for some reason, she felt disappointed by his response.

"You haven't always thought that have you?"

"No." Rupert hesitated before continuing, "After all, I gave up my life because of it."

"That's an interesting way to put it," she said smiling, but the expression on his face told her a lot more.

Athena studied the man before her who, despite his

attempts to hide it, appeared to be under some emotional stress. He twisted the ring on his right hand distractedly and occasionally raised his hand to his temple, pressing deeply as if hoping to obliterate his thoughts.

"Are you alright?" She was surprised by her own directness. He looked up quickly.

"I'm sorry. I've had a recent death in my family."

Athena gasped. When Rupert revealed that he had lost his twin brother, she was stunned. She thought of the form he had returned to her and realised why he had been reluctant to complete it.

He smiled apologetically and changed the tone of the conversation, sitting even straighter in his seat.

"You're doing your research at this university?"

Athena noticed his attempt to lighten the situation, but she felt uncomfortable talking about herself now and offered to make another time.

He seemed to be considering her offer, which she thought — she hoped — he would accept.

"Perhaps ..." He hesitated. "No, it might be best to do it now. I'll be taking some leave after this week."

She searched his face. "If you're sure that you're up to it, I would be most grateful."

Rupert smiled. He scanned the office while making his decision.

"I'm up to it," he said still smiling. "But do you mind if we move location? I think I need to get out of here."

"Certainly," she said, "Where would you like to go?"

"A walk?"

He was already standing, waiting for her.

"That sounds good," she said getting up and taking her coat from him.

Once outside the office, she turned to him and was again

aware of his height. In relative silence they walked down the two flights of stairs. At the building's entrance they were jostled by students, three abreast, entering for an afternoon lecture.

"Right or left?" Athena asked as shy strangers do when they can never assume to know the other's mind nor dare to choose for them.

"Left."

Rupert was embarrassed about his earlier display and that he had made Athena feel uncomfortable. It often seemed to be the way of late that he was taken unawares by a rising of emotion when he least expected or wanted it. He took her in out of the corner of his eye as they walked, noticing that when the sunlight caught her hair it was a combination of colours including red, a shade deeper than her coat. He had noticed a moment earlier, that same shade in the tips of her eyelashes.

They headed through the grounds of the university towards the river.

"Shall we begin?" Athena had stopped walking.

He paused and ran a hand through his hair, pondering the best way to begin.

"I think I probably need to tell you about my family circumstances at the time ... to put it into context."

"Does it have a context?" she said, a red-tinged eyebrow cocked in mock sarcasm.

"I think you'll see that it does," he answered her seriously, "which is why you might be disappointed, no, not disappointed, that's probably not the right word ... vindicated in your beliefs? Oh, I don't know."

"Let me be the judge of that."

He took a deep breath, and they resumed walking.

"Right … Anyway, our family life … Ross, my twin, and mine … was not a happy one. Our parents, well, there was a lot of bitterness there. They argued quite a bit of the time. Loud arguing."

"Do you mean violence?" Athena asked tentatively.

"No, not so much actual violence. More the threat of it if you know what I mean? That's almost as bad, I think. That feeling that it's going to happen at any minute."

She nodded.

"Well, that went on for many years. Our father was a very domineering man. Our mother … I suppose life would have been quieter if she didn't retaliate, but that's not right, is it? That one person should try to dominate like that. She was right to defend herself. She was a proud woman, a good mother and a good wife, if he let her be the woman she wanted to be. Not what he wanted her to be."

"She didn't leave him?"

"Oh no. She would never have broken up the family for the sake of her own freedom."

It pained him to think of what his mother had had to bear. She had been an intelligent woman; she had studied agricultural science and had had a promising future before marrying his father. Rupert knew her frustration. He remembered the rare occasions when he had been alone with his mother, on days home sick from school. She would make him tomato sandwiches, cut in quarters, and sit on his bed to talk. Before long she would be reminiscing about her youth, or she would go through his rock collection, explaining how each of the pieces were formed. Her lovely face would be sad and wistful, and he would touch her hand to reassure her, "It's okay, Mum."

"And your father?"

Rupert could feel a little twist of his stomach at the mention of his father.

"He was a Minister in the Anglican Church."

"Anglican Church! But ... I don't understand."

"I'll get to that," he promised. "He just couldn't understand that his wife was unfulfilled. It was the times I suppose, but it was very hard on our mother. She developed depression, and she drank. My father, intolerant at the best of times, showed less compassion for his wife than his parishioners. They argued more and more."

Athena looked down at the ground as she spoke, aware of this personal revelation.

"That must have been very hard for you and Ross."

Rupert nodded and remembered how he and Ross had pleaded with their mother to stop drinking as the arguing between their parents became more regular. Rupert realized now that she had probably been drinking for years but had hidden it from them. Her increasing frustration and sense of worthlessness in her husband's eyes only aggravated the problem, to the point that she could no longer conceal it.

"How old were you both then?" Athena said.

"I'd say from about ten onwards. I'm not really sure."

"How did you feel?"

Rupert noticed how gently she asked him questions.

"We hated it. But at least we had each other. Fortunately, we were the only children. I think ... I know that it affected Ross very deeply, for the rest of his life in fact."

"You were twins you said."

"Yes. Identical."

"Identical! That's interesting."

Athena stopped walking. Rupert stopped too.

"Why is that?" he said.

She seemed to be deep in thought and spoke slowly, "It means of course that you are ... were, genetically identical. The links between our genetic make-up and our emotions is not established but ..." She looked up at him apologetically. "It's just that this is my area of interest."

They continued walking. There was less traffic now on the path and it was much quieter.

"And I think this brings us to the point of our meeting," Rupert said as way of getting started.

"Really?" She stopped to face him, confused as to what the connection could be. "Tell me."

Her eyes are green, Rupert thought. He'd been certain that they were brown. They walked on, more slowly than before.

Rupert used the rhythm of the stroll to launch himself into this memory, though he wasn't sure what he thought of it anymore.

"When Ross and I were seventeen, and in our last year of school, we came home to find our mother drinking and she was ... rambling." Rupert closed his eyes briefly as he remembered their distress, sensing the trouble that lay ahead. "We tried to sober her up before our father came home. We were worried. He came home and was angrier than we had ever seen him. He was on the verge of hitting her. We think he would have, but Ross hit him first. I was sort of shielding Mum ... I didn't see it happen, but I heard Father hit the floor. Ross ran out. He was so angry ... and scared, I think. Mum was screaming. I lifted Father to the chair. He was all right, but bleeding from a cut on his mouth and he was cursing us. I don't think he knew which one of us it was in all the confusion. I put Mum to bed and Father just sat in the chair and wouldn't speak."

Rupert paused, feeling the unwelcome return of the emotion of that night. He breathed deeply as he walked to slow his thoughts. Out the corner of his eye he could see that Athena was listening with grave attention. He continued.

"When they were both asleep, I went out looking for Ross. He'd been gone for hours. I called at some friends' houses, but he wasn't there. Then I had this feeling of where he would be and ... he was there ... standing on the edge of the bluff close to our home where we often used to sit and talk. But it was dark. He had his back to me, and he was weaving about with a bottle of Mum's scotch that he must have hidden from her. I approached him slowly, I was afraid of what he was going to do ... I hadn't seen him like that before."

He stopped walking. Athena faced him silently.

"When I was close enough, I called his name. He turned around to face me, but he started to taunt me ... moving backwards to the edge of the bluff, his arms up high, and he kept swilling from that bloody bottle ..."

He stopped. "Sorry." In relating that night to Athena, he saw all too clearly where his brother's trouble had begun. He was never the same after it, and Rupert would continue to curse the bottles of alcohol that became Ross's constant accessories.

Athena smiled at him sympathetically.

"Anyway, he went on like that for a while and I was just ... frozen to the spot. I just kept telling him that I loved him and then, finally, he just fell down on his knees and cried his heart out."

Rupert's eyes smarted.

Athena looked down to the ground. He saw it and was grateful. He breathed deeply, conscious that he had spoken for a long time and still had not come to the point of his monologue. He was unaccustomed to speaking about himself at such length.

"I *will* get to the point," he said light-heartedly, trying to lift the intensity of the moment.

She looked up and smiled and Rupert thought she brushed his arm. She looked across to a nearby park bench.

"Do you want to sit down for it?" she said. "I think I need to."

"Good idea," he said, leading the way and disturbing a flock of seagulls feeding on chips that had been spilt on the ground.

He waited for her to sit before seating himself.

They sat quietly together staring ahead, each lost for a moment in their own thoughts. The river was calm and looked like mercury. A skiff passed by them silently, its rowers grimly intent in their task.

"So ..." Rupert laughed as he faced her. "This is going to be an anticlimax. I've told you the most dramatic part. I imagined that you would be ticking boxes and taking copious notes."

"I'll remember," she said, settling back into the bench as if in for the long haul. "I'm ready."

Looking ahead he noted how the water's surface had been sliced into two even parts, each rippling its way towards the banks. He focused his thoughts and spoke, much slower now.

"I went to him then ... to Ross ... and held him in my arms while he let it all out. We were just tired of it all you see. It had gone on so long, and we were constantly anxious. Ross fell asleep, probably helped by the alcohol, and I didn't have the heart to move him. So, we just stayed there, on the ground, by the edge of that bluff. It was quite late, but there was a full moon so I could see most things around me. I could hear the waves crashing on the shore below. It was peaceful. I was wide-awake, holding Ross, and probably thinking about it all ... I don't remember." He paused while he tried to think of a way to explain what happened next. "What I do remember is that I was looking at a nearby pine tree and I became aware of a ... visible clarity ... of the tree, of Ross, and, as I looked up and around at the stars, the moon, it was as if ... " Rupert searched his mind for something that would help to explain his experience, " ... as if everything had suddenly taken on a heightened reality. And then ..." He took a long intake of air through his nose before continuing. "It all became indistinguishable points of vibrating light. I couldn't define any one thing from another — not even my hands."

He stopped abruptly and looked at her, trying to gauge her reaction.

Athena had been watching him intently while he spoke, and her eyes had widened. He thought he saw her shiver.

"That's not all I'm afraid," he said almost apologetically.

"Oh?"

"There was something else." This was the part he was dreading the most. "A voice." He looked down and could feel himself blush.

"Oh," she said.

He continued slowly, "When I say a voice, it was ... in my head, not something that anyone else would have heard."

"What did it say?"

"Well ... It's difficult. It was more the feeling that I had ... an incredible, *indescribable* feeling of peace that was overwhelming. I felt like I was physically fusing with everything around me ... and I knew that I was being called to serve him."

She looked confused.

Rupert continued. "I knew, well, at the time I thought I knew, that it was the voice of God, wanting, asking me to live my life in his service. There were no particular words I can recall, as I said, more a feeling."

He had often thought about it over the years, tried to rationalize it, but he had held a deep conviction that the experience, that the voice, was real, not imagined. That is, until now.

"Why would you assume it was an experience of God?"

Although Athena still looked bemused, she listened intently.

"I ask myself that now, but, at the time, I had no doubt that it was God. As the son of a Minister, I had grown up with religion. When I look back, I don't think I could have thought it was anything else."

"And so you became a priest. Did you want to? Had you thought about it before?"

"Not really, and ... no. But I felt at the time that I couldn't deny that call." He stopped for a moment, her silence suggesting that she needed time to digest it. "I told you it would sound trite."

"No, no. It doesn't sound trite at all! It's just, I suppose I would understand better if I had an experience myself." She considered for a little longer. "But why the Catholics?"

Rupert laughed. "I think I was rebelling against my father. There were several factors. A chance meeting with a Catholic priest." His heart lifted at the thought of Matthew, his dearest friend and mentor. "An idea about the significance of celibacy, which was probably disguising a resolve not to marry, and yes ... some rebellion."

"What about Ross?" Athena said. "What happened after that incident?"

"That night marked the beginning of a downward spiral. He was angry, with me, of course, for making my decision. He couldn't understand it and I think he felt that I had abandoned him. He managed to complete an engineering degree and did quite well considering he was rarely at lectures, usually sleeping off a hangover. Then, when we were twenty-five, he met and married Kate."

He could feel a small surge of anger at the thought of his former sister-in-law. Kate had been a student of Fine Arts at the same university when Ross and Rupert were studying. Finely strung, but talented and creative, she lived the life of a bohemian artist, and Ross had fallen madly in love with her.

"Was it a happy marriage?"

"No. Well, it was at first, but Kate had some problems of her own and she ... she didn't help his problems. They divorced several years ago."

"And there were no children?"

"Yes. One. Neti, my niece."

"And she's with her mother?"

Rupert paused, knowing that this was the root of his anger towards Kate. Though it was obvious that domestic life stifled her, she had had a child with Ross and then abandoned them when Neti was just five years old. Rupert could never understand how she could walk away from her family.

"No. Neti's with me."

Athena looked confused.

"Kate left Ross and Neti ten years ago," Rupert explained. "She broke my brother's heart. Despite their difficulties, he loved her."

"So, he was left to raise Neti ... and now?"

"I'm her guardian. There's no one else. We don't have any other family, and she's Ross's daughter, my niece, I should raise her."

"You can do that as a priest?"

"It's not usual. But these are not usual circumstances."

"How's it going?"

"It's a learning process."

"I'll bet!" Athena laughed.

They sat silently for a while, staring at the passing boat, lost in their own thoughts.

Rupert looked at his watch. He needed to shop for dinner and made his apologies.

Athena stood up with him.

"Would it be an imposition if I talked with you again, about the details?"

Rupert considered this for a moment. For the first time in a while, he felt a little lighter. He already knew that he would like to speak with her again. She had been very patient, and it had been much easier than he had thought to tell her of his experience. He reminded her that he would be taking leave.

"I'll contact you later this week?" she offered.

Something about her made him smile. "That's probably the best. Can I walk you back?"

"No, thank you. I might stay here for a bit longer. Rupert, thanks for sharing your experience with me."

"I hope it was helpful."

"I'm sure it will be. I'll be in touch."

Rupert hesitated for a moment, feeling that he would like to say more.

"Goodbye, then."

"Ciao," Athena called after Rupert. It had been difficult for him to tell her about this episode in his life, and she was grateful to him for the effort he made on her behalf. There was plenty of material there to inform her research and she was excited; she would record it immediately when she returned to her office. But as she wandered back through the grounds of the university, it was not the material that she pondered. Something about this man lingered. His gentleness and vulnerability had made her want to reach out to him. He had moved her. Though it bemused her, Athena knew that with Rupert's leaving, she had experienced a small sense of loss.

Rupert walked from the train station, carrying the ingredients for the recipe on page 21 of his new cookbook *Family Meals with a Difference*. Two doors from home he could hear the throb of Neti's stereo. He could feel himself becoming agitated, partly because of the volume of the music, but more in anticipation of her mood.

He opened the front door, the thump of the music so intense it almost sent him reeling backwards. As he came through the room, he saw four girls, including Neti, lying around on the couch and floor, the air faintly hazy with the smoke of cigarettes.

"Hello," he said to one girl who looked up and saw him.

She jumped up immediately and looked nervously around at the others. She headed to the stereo and turned the music down.

"Hello," he said again, this time audibly to all four girls.

"Hi ... Hello ... Hi", Neti's friends responded, but she remained expressionless and silent.

Rupert surveyed the scene that was littered with chip packets, the contents of several spilling onto the floor, glasses of Coke and a half-filled ashtray. He was on the verge of saying something — about the volume of the music, the cigarettes, the use of time after school, but Neti's unruffled demeanour suggested that she was waiting for him to do just that.

"How are you girls?" he said instead, and then to Neti, "I'll have dinner ready in about an hour."

"Fine," she said.

She turned back to her friends to resume their conversation. They looked at her and then to him uncertainly.

"Anyway," Neti said forcefully, pressuring them to continue.

Rupert took his leave of them. He unpacked the shopping bags on the kitchen bench. Mercifully, the volume was not turned up again, but he could hear their lowered voices punctuated now and then by Neti's raucous laugh. He felt sad when he heard that. He knew he was the topic of conversation, but Neti's attitude towards him hurt him deeply. It hadn't always been like that. As Ross's brother, and possibly even more because he was his twin, Rupert had spent a lot of time with Ross and Neti over the years, particularly since Kate had left. He had spent every birthday with her, every Christmas and even the occasional holiday. He always considered that he had a very good relationship with Neti, and he loved her. There was no doubt that he felt some awkwardness with children and particularly teenagers, but it had never really posed any problems before. He realised that Ross probably acted as the buffer between their profound differences and Neti was now becoming increasingly belligerent towards him.

Since her father's death, Neti had shown very little emotion — at least publicly. She didn't know that he heard her crying in her room on several occasions, but any attempt of his to talk with her about it was met with derision. He knew that she had to cope with it in her own way, but he was concerned that she would not talk about it, nor express her sorrow, and it was now manifesting in reckless behaviour. He smelt cigarette smoke coming from her room on several occasions and Neti's appearance was becoming more dishevelled. She rarely put out her washing, or did it herself, and Rupert was reluctant to trespass in her room to collect it.

He opened the recipe book. Marjorie had suggested that the way to Neti's heart might be through her stomach. He had been unconvinced, given that the healthy but simple fare that he had been cooking for her usually ended in the compost. Marjorie smiled at him in amusement when he told her this. Neti's probably bored, she had said. Marjorie had also quipped that it might do both of them good to be a little more adventurous with meals. Shopping had been an adventure, Rupert thought, as he scanned the exotic ingredients before him, but he had to admit to the pleasure he derived from wandering the market stalls and to the anticipation of cooking Neti a meal she might enjoy.

He concentrated on the recipe before him, anxious to measure and chop and grind exactly as instructed — the highly coloured photograph of the Thai Chicken and Singapore Noodles he was attempting to cook intimidated him. At different moments, when he could afford to let his mind wander, the events of the afternoon rose to the surface of his thoughts.

It had surprised him how easy it was to tell Athena about his experience: *the* experience. Her self-assuredness and air of strength and reliability had made it easier for him to tell her. In fact, he had told her more than he had originally intended, more than he might normally say, except perhaps to Marjorie or to Ross. Since Marjorie had given him the envelope, Rupert had thought about what had happened to him on the night that now seemed so long ago. Remembering how certain he had been of his experience did not produce the same certainty in him now. He viewed it cynically and reasoned that it had been his own youthful enthusiasm and need at the time that had interpreted it as something profound. In another sense, though, he longed to feel it again, in fact, to feel an enthusiasm for anything at all.

Athena could be trusted, he thought. Other thoughts came too; not to do with what he or she said, but gestures and movements and facial expressions.

An hour later, Neti's girlfriends had left. He put his head in the lounge room. She was lying on the couch watching a game show on television. He noticed that she had made no attempt to clean up the room.

"Dinner's ready for those who are game."

He knew that she would resist sitting at the kitchen table to eat. The first few nights together became a tense battle of wills about where to eat the meal. She insisted that Ross had allowed her to eat on the couch while watching the television. Although he knew it would be easier if he just let her do so, and he would also have some peace, he felt that the evening meal was the only time that he could make any real contact. Not that any valuable contact had been made as yet. So far, they had spent each meal in an uncomfortable silence, dotted with stilted small talk.

Surprisingly, she didn't raise an objection, but merely slouched reluctantly to the kitchen. She flopped into the chair and waited for her meal to be served to her. Rupert, bringing the plates over from the bench, noticed how white the skin of her neck was since she had had her hair cut very short. Despite her bravado, she was really just a child, he thought.

He placed her meal in front of her, holding his breath, while she studied it. He'd followed the instructions exactly, right down to the garnish of coriander leaves and felt some pride that it did resemble the photograph.

"What's this?" she said yawning.

"Thai chicken. I've never made it before."

"No kidding. What's the green stuff?"

"Do you mean in it or on top of it?"

"Both."

"It's coriander on top and green curry in with the chicken."

"Curry!"

"It shouldn't be too hot," he said quickly as he sat down, "but there's water here if it is."

He picked up his fork to begin. She sat staring at the plate for a moment but then picked up her fork and made small stabbing movements at the edges of her meal. She gave a small grimace after her first mouthful, but Rupert was relieved to see her go back for a second and a third.

"Neti, I think we need to talk about what happens after school."

"What do you mean?" she said looking up from her meal. Her tone indicated that he was treading on treacherous ground. For a moment, he wished he hadn't raised it, but he felt the need to pursue the matter of this afternoon.

"It's fine to have your friends over at the weekend of course, but I think that you should really do a few hours of homework when you get home. You must have quite a bit?"

"No."

"I find that hard to believe."

"Please yourself. They don't give us any. Anyway, I do it at school."

"I noticed that someone had been smoking this afternoon."

"So? Kate and Jane are allowed to. They smoke at home."

"Well, that may be the case, but I don't think that they should be smoking here."

She looked at him directly.

"Dad used to let them."

He put down his fork.

"Neti, I know it must be hard for you, and I know that I'm not Dad—"

There was a knock at the front door. Neti jumped up to answer it, eager to get away. She came back in a few moments later looking bored and, he thought, disappointed.

"It's that woman you work with."

She plopped herself down again at the table and continued eating her dinner.

"Oh?" Rupert wiped his mouth with his serviette and went out to see who it was that Neti had left at the door.

"Marjorie!"

"Hello." She was holding a casserole dish that looked heavy. "I hope I haven't come at a bad time."

"Not at all, come in."

She handed him the dish.

"I thought you might like ... I just whipped up a casserole for you both."

He took it from her and dropped his arms in exaggeration of its weight.

"A hearty one by the feel of it. Thank you. You needn't have done that."

"That's all right. By the time I cook for all my family, it's just as easy to make two as one."

Rupert led the way towards the kitchen. Marjorie followed.

"I'll put this in the fridge for tomorrow night. Neti and I were just finishing tonight's attempt. Neti, do you remember Marjorie?"

Neti looked up from her plate.

"Yes. Hi."

"Doesn't that look delicious! Who cooked that?" Marjorie smiled at Rupert knowingly.

Neti picked up her nearly empty plate and took it to the sink.

"I was trying something new," Rupert said mockingly as he placed the casserole in the fridge.

Neti began to rinse the dishes noisily. Rupert raised an eyebrow to Marjorie.

"It's okay Neti, I'll do them later. You might want to just clean up the lounge room though."

"Whatever," she said over her shoulder as she left the kitchen.

"Mmmm ... How's it going?" Marjorie said once Neti was out of earshot.

"We get on like a house on fire," Rupert said, laughing.

"Yes, I can see the sparks flying."

"I didn't see you today," she said.

"I was in earlier, but I had an afternoon appointment — with the neuroscientist."

Marjorie looked concerned.

"What's wrong?"

Rupert laughed. "Nothing. *The* neuroscientist. The one you wanted me to talk to. Remember?"

"You *did* respond! Good on you. How did it go?"

"All right."

"What did she think of it?"

"I think she thinks I'm a complete nutter."

"Rupert."

"I don't know. What can you make of something like that?"

"Quite a lot I would say. You had a very profound experience that meant something very important to you once. Don't make light of it now."

"Hmm ... Have a seat. Cup of tea?"

"No, thanks. You need to finish your meal." She nudged him gently with her elbow. "Well done by the way. It looks as though you won Neti with that one."

"I wish it was that easy."

Rupert walked Marjorie to the door.

"Goodbye Neti, nice to see you again," Marjorie addressed the feet that were facing her over the top of the couch.

"Yeah ... Bye," came a voice from under a cushion. Neti's eyes remained fixed to the 7:30 sitcom.

Rupert rolled his eyes to Marjorie who bit her lower lip in amusement. He walked her to her car.

"Thanks for bringing the casserole," he said, opening her door.

"A pleasure. But I don't think I can compete with your cooking now."

"Ha!" he said. "I'll see you tomorrow."

She turned to him and kissed his forehead.

"You're a gentle man, Ru."

"I'm glad someone likes me," he said returning the kiss.

When he came back inside, Neti was still riveted to the television, occasionally letting out a roar of laughter that seemed somewhat exaggerated. He knew what that meant. It was a warning — to keep his distance and not pursue the earlier conversation.

He knew that he *should* pursue it, but he was tired and wanted some peace.

He sat down adjacent to her, pretending at first to be watching the programme too.

"Neti," he said finally. "I'd like to talk to you."

She groaned loudly and rolled so that her back was to him, her face hidden in the couch and the pillow brought up to cover her exposed ear.

Rupert turned down the volume on the television.

"Neti."

"What *now*?" She flung her body around to face him.

Rupert tried not to look too ruffled. He knew that this was a ploy to keep him off-guard and it had worked before. He kept his voice as even as possible.

"I'm concerned about you at the moment."

She didn't answer him but rolled onto her back and stared at the ceiling.

He continued. "I know it must be hard for you at the moment—"

"I'm fine," she cut in abruptly.

Rupert swallowed and pursued his line, "I could never replace your father, Neti, and I don't want to ..."

He could see that her chin was starting to quiver, but her eyes remained unflinchingly set on the ceiling.

"I just want us to try to work together. To make the best of the situation ... I do love you."

"*Leave it alone!*" She jumped up from the couch and stormed to the kitchen, still clutching the cushion.

Tentatively, he followed her. She was bending over the sink, holding her stomach and sobbing.

"Neti ..." He moved towards her.

"*Go away!*" She turned to him, her face pinched and mottled.

Despite her protestations, Rupert went to her and held her. Surprisingly, she didn't resist and let herself cry into his chest.

Eventually, when she had drained herself of tears, Neti broke away from his grasp, not aggressively, but hesitantly, as if there was a tug-of-war between her emotions.

"Could I run a bath for you?" Rupert offered helplessly, uncertain what to say next.

He thought of his mother and how, after she and his father had had another row, she would run a bath for Rupert and Ross when they were young, in a desperate attempt to soothe them as if nothing had happened, as if every family behaved this way and it could easily be remedied. And Rupert and Ross would each take his turn dipping into the healing water. It would work for Rupert, with the door closed, head submerged, tapping on the side of the bath pretending he was in a submarine, and blowing giant soap bubbles from between his arms. He remembered that he was always first in, but Ross insisted it be so. Rupert knew that it was because Ross would pee in the bath — he liked the injection of warmth when the bath had cooled down.

Rupert smiled his first smile at the memory of his brother.

Neti did not want a bath, the offer brought a look of bemusement to her face, but, for the first time since they had lived together, her goodnight was not said through a hardened jaw. She did not want to talk, Rupert could see that, but she hesitated at the kitchen door and, though she kept her back to him, he could hear her say it, softly and with some meaning.

"Hello, Rupert?"

"Yes."

"Athena Nevis speaking."

"Hello Athena."

His voice sounded genuinely friendly, though she was anxious not to upset him when he was obviously still grieving.

"I hope I haven't called you at a bad time," she said, thinking too that it was nice to hear his voice.

"No, not at all. I'm almost there with my lesson plans etcetera. What did you conclude?" he said with a hint of amusement. "Am I as mad as the rest?"

"Madder."

"Just as I thought," he said with a laugh. "Can I help you further or did you just want to confirm what I already knew?"

She laughed at his quip, thinking that he sounded much lighter than last time they met. She felt then a rising sense of anxiety.

"There are a few things I would like to ask you if you have time, about your brother, and your mother, but I would understand if it's too painful at the moment."

He was silent at the other end. *Damn*, she thought to herself, regretting the words almost as soon as she had said them. But his voice came back still as bright as before.

"All right, but I don't have much time this week. Unless we meet today?"

"Oh, that would be great," she said, taken by surprise. "Shall I come to your office?"

"I haven't had lunch yet. Could we talk and eat? Would that be too informal?"

She was further surprised and wished she could say something else other than, "Great."

They arranged to meet in an hour at the cafeteria least frequented by students.

Athena caught herself smiling as she put down the receiver.

She recognized the lean frame in the blue cable knit jumper, sitting at an outdoor table. As she approached him from behind, she noticed that his hair swirled a little at the crown.

When she came around to face him, his eyes were closed as he soaked up the meagre sunlight. She would have loved to have taken him in then, without him seeing her, but she panicked at the thought of being caught in the act. She coughed.

He opened his eyes instantly and looked directly into her face, which startled her.

"Hi," she said guiltily.

"Hello again," he said standing up to greet her. "Is it too cold to sit out here?"

"No," she said sitting. "How are you?"

"Well, thanks." Rupert said smiling and eyeing the notepad, pen and glasses that Athena was placing on the table. "This looks intimidating. I'm going to be committed to print now, am I?"

Athena blushed. "I've already recorded the experience as you related it," Athena reassured him, "But there are a couple of questions ... as I mentioned."

"Yes," he said, but Athena thought she could see his eyes cloud over a little. "Ask away."

"Rupert, are you sure you're up to this?" She felt a rise of panic about the questions she needed to ask and how they would make him feel.

"Ask away," he said again, but this time more softly.

"Your brother," she began tentatively, "did he drink before that night?"

"Well, yes, as I had, socially with our friends. Why? Is it important?" Rupert did not look distressed but seemed perplexed by her question.

"There is some interesting material to consider," she continued. "That night you told me about, it seems to have been important for you both in that you each had a significant experience, albeit different in nature and effect."

"You think the cause was the same?" Rupert seemed to be following Athena's line of reasoning.

She nodded in agreement. "I'm not a psychologist, however my study is linked to psychology. The episodes of that night, with your parents, may have triggered something in each of you that led to your brother's alcoholism and ... perhaps your experience of heightened perception."

Rupert seemed to be deep in thought.

Athena continued, "Of course, it's not that simple. You may have each taken your paths in life regardless. It's just so interesting that you and your brother were identical twins and that could have provided a wealth of information ..."

"If he hadn't died you mean."

The statement was made matter-of-factly enough, but Athena eyed Rupert to be sure that she was not treading on too sensitive ground.

"Identical twins provide such a wonderful opportunity to learn about the relationship between our genetic make-up and behaviour: the old nature-nurture debate. My work involves looking at the possibility that our genes determine our brain chemistry, in conjunction with our lifestyle, which, in turn, manifests our personalities."

"And alcoholism?" Rupert said, looking confused.

"There is evidence that there is a genetic predisposition."

Rupert's eyes widened. "I see. That's why you're interested in my mother?"

Athena nodded. "Yes. It suggests the possibility of an inheritance factor."

"You use a lot of 'possibilities'," Rupert said smiling, but the change in conversation was not lost on Athena. "Milk?"

She studied his reaction. She knew that this was a sensitive area, and her suggestions might be construed as trite explanations for some of the behaviour of people Rupert loved.

"Yes. That's both the frustration and the challenge of science," she answered him, "stepping from the 'possible' to the 'actual'."

"Do you think that everything can be explained by science?" Rupert was genuinely interested.

"Y ... yes. Ultimately, I'm sure we will be able to explain everything."

"What about love?" His face was blank as he poured her tea.

Athena could feel the colour rise in her face. "Do I believe in it? Yes. Do I think that neuroscience will be able to explain the emotion? Yes ..."

"If what you are saying proves to be true," Rupert said thoughtfully over the rim of his cup, "that is, that spiritual experiences, beliefs and love are explainable in this way, what effect do you think this knowledge might have?"

"On?" Athena said uncertainly, between bites of her sandwich.

"Those who believe that such things are transcendent?" Rupert's face was earnest and the expression in his eyes suggested to Athena that the answer was most important to him.

"Are you talking generally or are you talking about yourself?" she said. "Perhaps you can answer that."

"Do you believe in God?" he asked her directly.

"I have never felt the need," she said, but wished that she had phrased it more diplomatically.

"Feeling the need is not enough, believe me."

Athena was taken aback at how bluntly he made the statement, but he looked away as her eyes searched his face.

"I would imagine that, considering your recent loss, you would be feeling numb."

He sipped his tea slowly while considering his answer.

"No ... I felt that immediately after Ross died. Now, I feel ... empty."

She was aware that this was a large admission and sensed the need to provide an opportunity to continue.

"If you talk about it, you might have more feelings than you think."

He sighed with resignation and placed the cup back on the table. "It's not the emptiness that's bothering me. There was a time when I seemed to have unlimited access to the 'Grace of God' for want of a better term, and I could draw on that in moments of crisis. I felt the emptiness when our mother died but my faith enabled me to pull through. This is different. Now I feel there is nothing to access."

"What changed?" Athena's voice softened.

"Me."

As he spoke, she noticed the tips of his fingers turning white as they exerted pressure on the edge of the table.

"I don't think I believe anymore."

"But you've devoted your life to believing in a god!" Athena's eyes widened. "How could you do that unless you were very sure?"

She searched his face for clues to the extent of his dilemma. He was sitting back into the seat, his head down. "It's easy enough to go through the motions. I've spent so long convincing my students that there must be a 'Grand Design', I'd assumed that I was convinced of it myself."

Athena leaned towards him. She noticed that swirl of hair that looked untamed, almost defiant against his careful combing.

"But you have just lost someone very close to you. Of course, you're feeling confused!"

He looked at her steadily.

"It's more than that. I'm not just caught up in my emotions, abusing God for abandoning me. I feel nothing. Except, perhaps, the rising sense of my own stupidity — that I've given up my life for nothing. The joke's on me!" He raised the cup in a mock toast and brought it to his lips. "You must agree?"

The note of sarcasm was not lost on her.

"The difference is that I have never believed."

"Then you must see me as a fool" he replied quickly.

"No ... I see you as being lost."

Athena could hear the indignation rising in his voice.

"Why lost? Neither of us is a believer!"

She sensed that she had probably gone too far. This was someone she hardly knew after all and she was treading on obviously sensitive personal ground. There was something in his pain that made her want to help him. She had an urge to reach across the table and grab his hand, but she knew that that would be inappropriate and resisted.

She said instead, "There is a desolation in your voice ... because of what you had, your belief, and now you don't have it anymore. That's the difference between us."

"Have you ever lost anyone?" Rupert asked, his tone softening in response to her.

"No ... yes ... grandparents, a dog, a cat ..."

He smiled. "It's a joke, isn't it? We live. We die. For what?"

"It's just the way it is," Athena replied.

"But doesn't that disturb you? That there is no point. That there is no single reason why we should act justly or why we should even care what we do to anyone else. Except, perhaps, to keep ourselves out of prison!"

"Why does there have to be a point?" This time it was Athena's turn to be indignant. "Why does there have to be a bigger meaning, a purpose, for doing the right thing?" She leant across the table to make her point. "Why can't you just do it because it's the responsible thing to do! No rewards! Just do it because we're all in this life together and we have responsibility to each other!"

She could feel her tone rising and sank back away from it into her seat. "Don't get me wrong," she said more gently, "I don't want to die or to lose the people I love, but it's all part of being here. We live, we *love,*" she emphasised the part he had forgotten, "we die. That's beautiful enough, isn't it?"

Athena knew her face would be flushed, and she looked away. When she looked at him again, he was watching her.

"I'm sorry," he said with a gentle smile. "You came to ask me questions for your research, and I have taken the time with my own concerns."

"I think I probably have enough," Athena said, still embarrassed about her little tirade and reluctant to pursue her agenda any further.

"But you didn't get to take anything down," Rupert said, eyeing the notepad and pen that were still lying on the table.

"I have a good memory," she joked. She shuffled them into her bag and took out her purse. "I'd better let you get back to your work," she said standing. "Let me get this, please."

Before he could answer she went inside to pay. When she came back, he was standing, waiting for her. Once again, she felt a sense of anxiety, but she wasn't sure what the cause was this time.

"You shouldn't have done that," he said, "I should have paid you for listening to me. I owe you now ..." He looked down at his feet and said quickly, "dinner, or something."

He cocked his head sheepishly and she could see that he was blushing.

"With Neti, my niece, if that's all right."

"That would be lovely," she said.

"I'll call you then? When we're organised?"

"Yes. Call me then," she reassured him. She tore a piece of paper from her notepad and wrote her telephone number. "I got to write something after all," she said laughing.

CHAPTER FOUR

Dear Ru

How long has it been, Dear Heart?

Before your letter arrived bearing its grim news, I would have said that it was a millennium since we last met. Since I have read of the tragedy, so gently written in your dear handwriting, it is but a beat of a cicada's wing.

Poor, dear Ross. What happened to his life Rupert? His dreams?

Rupert sat back from the letter and closed his eyes. His fingers twitched at the paper's edge. He took an agitated breath and continued reading.

I can only imagine the extent of your pain. But I, more than others, would know the depth and strength of your bond. I'm sure that I don't have to remind you of that Rupert. You and your twin were, after all, one who became two.

*I fear for you at this time. I know how you can suffer, and I
suspect that you will not be taking this well (although I have no
doubt that you are presenting a stoic face to the world).*

Rupert felt a bubble of rage rise upward.

*I have thought about your anguish constantly Ru and realise the
impossible burden that has been placed upon you. I must return
to my baby girl and take up the responsibility that is mine and
which you so unselfishly took on as your own.*

I am her mother and Neti needs me now.

*I'll arrive next Tuesday to pick up the pieces of my daughter's
life and give you back yours.*

*Until then, Love and Peace
Kat.*

Rupert tossed the letter across the bed and leant back on
the pillow and the hard headboard. He stared at the woven
lightshade on the ceiling, realising that it was the product of his
sister-in-law's handy work, as were, no doubt, many other items
decorating this room in which he now slept. He was not going
to be able to dismiss her as easily as he did the letter.

She *can't* come. She *mustn't* come.

He felt a surge of panic as adrenalin flooded his blood.
There was an ominous tone to the letter that disturbed him and
that could not be disguised by the sentiments expressed.
Although her record might have given him hope that this was a
bluff, or a spur of the moment sense of duty that would die out
as quickly as it began, he felt her presence threateningly close.

Why now? His anxiety turned to anger. If she had wanted

to come home, why didn't she do it years ago? Then, perhaps, his brother would be alive.

But he knew that Kate would never have come home to Ross. Their differences were irreconcilable. Ross could not face this fact; when he did, he washed it away with alcohol.

His thoughts calmed. Perhaps she genuinely wanted to return to her daughter, and she could only do this without Ross's presence. Her desertion, her failure to communicate or to make any effort to see Neti, had been Ross's greatest weapon. Although he had desperately wanted his wife to return, his sorrow turned to bitterness, and he held onto Neti fiercely.

And if she really did want to come home, perhaps it would be the best thing. Neti would have her mother and he could go back to the life he had known for twenty years. Strangely, the thought gave him no pleasure at all. He picked up the letter again and considered Kate's signature.

'Kat'. How long had she been known by that name? The letter aimed at an intimacy they had shared and yet she had signed it with a name he could not relate to. But the superficial tone of the letter, and the signature, confirmed for him that she had been living out her alternative lifestyle dreams. In a way, he applauded her for it. She had always been 'out of step' with mainstream life. It was what had attracted Ross to her in the beginning.

"Next Tuesday." It was already Thursday. She wasn't wasting any time.

Sounds of the opening and closing of the refrigerator door brought him back to his prime concern. Neti never spoke of her mother, nor her father, now, not to Rupert at least. How was he going to tell her? Would she feel abandoned by him too? Perhaps he was fooling himself that he meant anything in his niece's life. She showed few positive sentiments towards him anymore, and, despite his best efforts, her behaviour and appearance were becoming increasingly erratic.

He was failing her. And yet, in his heart, he felt that he was the only constant person in her life providing her, he hoped, with some sense of security and continuity.

"Damn her," he cursed his thoughts of Kate to the walls of the room she had decorated a decade before.

Although he wished he could put it off, he readied himself to tell Neti.

"Hungry?" he said tentatively as he put his head into the kitchen. The rest of his body followed slowly, the hand holding Kate's letter the last part of him to come through the door.

She ignored him.

"I'll be cooking dinner soon. I thought I'd just have a read of the mail first."

She raised her eyebrows as if wishing that he would say nothing at all.

"There is a letter ..." he said somewhat nervously, raising the letter.

"How nice for you," she said with her back to him.

"It's from Kate, your mother."

He hadn't meant it to come out so bluntly. Neti swung around, the ingredients of the sandwich she was making flying in all directions.

It pained him to look at her. She didn't look horrified as he had expected. Instead, her eyes were bright, and her face was flushed. He should have been happy for her, but he wasn't.

"My mother? What does she say?"

She moved towards him as if to grab the letter with her free hand, the sandwich dangling precariously in the other.

He stepped back and opened it out to read.

"She's coming next Tuesday."

Neti's eyebrows were raised so high they were straining under her surprise.

Rupert had to hold his tongue for fear that he would reveal his cynicism.

"She wants to come home to you. To look after you," he said instead. He could feel his body twitching with the tension of his false sincerity.

"I *knew* it!"

Neti flung the forgotten snack onto the bench.

"Could I read it?" she said with a look that demanded compliance.

He handed it to her. She poured over its contents obviously savouring every word. He felt like an intruder.

He walked past her to the refrigerator and took out the ingredients for dinner. Neti, not aware of his presence anymore, headed to her room still reading her mother's words.

"Dinner won't be long," he called after her feebly.

The only sound that answered him was the soft click as she closed her bedroom door behind her.

Once on her bed, her sanctuary, Neti straightened the creases from the paper and reread it, marvelling at her mother's hand-writing and the unusual way she expressed herself. This was the first intimate contact she had had with her that she could remember, except for the Luck Bird. She took it from the bedside table and faced it to the letter.

"You brought this," she said to the cloth bird in admiration. "I knew she would come home," she said to the walls.

"Tuesday, Tuesday ..." She counted the days on her fingers. "Five days!"

Suddenly she felt nervous. She jumped up from the bed

WHISPERS IN THE WIRING

and peered into the mirror of her dressing table. She plucked at her spiky locks trying to soften them. She rummaged through a box of hair accessories and produced two tortoiseshell combs which she swiped through her hair trying to tame it.

"Blah, you loser!" She insulted her image.

She turned away then looked back sharply as if trying to catch her reflection in the act of doing something it shouldn't. She only ever just got a tiny bit of the eye's white. She tried it again and again, half expecting that one day her image's eyes would be a second behind her own and she could say "Hah ... Got you!"

She laughed at herself and was so pleased with the effect she laughed some more, trying out different tones and expressions — silly laughs, sophisticated laughs, testing each to find one that she would take on as her own.

"Hello mu ..." She stopped mid rehearsal, realising that she did not know how to address her own mother.

"Hello mother." No. Too formal. "Hello mum." Too familiar.

"Hello Kat, nice to see you." She extended her hand to the mirror in a gesture of welcome, her head thrown back as if waiting for her hand to be kissed by a royal suitor.

"Dickhead," she said laughing.

Rupert could not bear the thought of meeting Kate in the place he had last seen her. Too much had happened. To just walk back in the door would be to stake a claim he felt she had no right to. He wanted her to know the full thumping force of his anger and he could not do that in the house in which he was, to Kate and Neti, a guest.

He had expected a strong reaction to his letter of reply. He had suggested that he meet her at Southern Cross Station when her train arrived, that way he could buy some time, assess her, before she reclaimed Neti.

She replied with a brief telephone call, simply informing him of the time of her arrival: no questions or platitudes. Her voice propelled him back in time. This contraction reinforced his anxiety about her stepping into the house she had left behind, that it would make a mockery of Ross's death and all the pain in the intervening years.

He felt calm, almost vacant, as he waited on the station for her train to pull in. He was tired of anticipating this meeting. Too many things contributed to his weariness. Undoubtedly, his concern for Neti was the most taxing. Since receiving her mother's letter, she had changed from dark and brooding to too cheerful, almost hyperactive. Her reaction to him had converted from a resigned resentment of his presence to an off-hand dismissal of him, no doubt brought on by the prospect of his departure. She had even taken to cleaning the house in an effort, he suspected, to sterilise what was soon to be the past.

Rupert's impending move, back to the residential college, raised another concern of which he had not been aware. How could he return to the life he knew before? He had not fully realised that living in his brother's house was providing a distraction from his inner spiritual turmoil. Although he still performed his religious duties, he did so mechanically. But there was nothing else that he could do. He was unqualified for life it seemed. For the first time in his life, he felt that he did not belong anywhere.

As the Brisbane-to-Melbourne pulled into the station, Rupert felt that he was watching his fate approach him and that there was little that he could do to alter its course.

There was a twenty-second pause before the passengers

alighted — enough time for him to unlock his knees and to move towards the main points of exit.

He didn't have to look too hard for her. She saw him first and was waving to him as she stepped down onto the platform.

"Ru! Ru!" she called to him as she threaded her way across the passengers who were herding to the departure gate.

She put down the larger bag she was carrying between her pair of scuffed cream midi-heels and his pair of polished black lace-ups and threw her arms around his neck.

"Oh Ru," she said stepping back to look at him, her hands still on his shoulders. His own arms hung by his side.

"You look so pale, you poor darling," she said pressing herself to him again.

Rupert stood unmoved initially but raised one hand in a feeble attempt to pat the back of her heavy woollen coat.

"Hello Kate," he said to her closest ear. He stepped away and she withdrew her arms self-consciously. He bent to pick up the bag, overcome with a sudden wave of anxiety.

"That's all my luggage," she said, slightly embarrassed and hitching the strap of her smaller handbag further onto her shoulder.

"The car's not far." He ushered her through the gate. "Did you have a good trip?" He was not yet looking at her eye to eye and wondered why he was the one to avert his gaze.

"I hate that trip," she said as she followed his lead.

Her comment caused him to wonder if she had made this journey several times before, without her family knowing.

She continued quickly, "I thought Neti might have come."

"She's at school," he said rather abruptly.

Neti had been adamant that she wanted to meet her mother too. Fortunately, she had a Drama rehearsal that she could not miss. As Drama was the one subject that she was committed to, Rupert did not have to force the issue.

"School ..." Kate's voice trailed off in wonder.

"Year Ten," he said.

After a long pause, she said, "How is she, Ru?"

"Taking it hard I think," he said, still a half pace in front of her.

"Yes, I suppose I could have given her more warning."

She had mistaken his meaning.

"Her father's death," he said quickly, not able to disguise his irritation.

He could sense her embarrassment.

"Ru, I'm sorry to hear about Ross." Her hand was on his arm.

He still could not look at her.

"We all are," he said, unlocking the passenger door of the white Cortina.

"Still got this car?" She searched his face for any kind of response. "I'll have the bag here," she said as he was about to close the door.

When he was about to start the engine, she turned to him.

"Please Ru ... talk to me."

He took his hand from the key and faced her. She was so close he could see unfamiliar lines etched into her face that she had tried to soften with make-up. Most noticeable were the vertical lines running down to her top lip. Her hair was blonder than he had remembered but was still full of soft curls framing her much thinner face. Her eyes, always her most striking feature, seemed bluer than ever, but they were older and had lost their fire. Although her clothes were clean, she looked dishevelled, but he assumed that it was the result of the long train journey.

He turned away from her and spoke to the windshield.

"What do you want me to say, Kate?"

He could take this opportunity to let it out as he imagined he would, but he was finding it difficult to organise the words.

"Anything! Say anything ... but don't treat me like a stranger." She was arching her body around to draw his face in her direction.

"In some ways you are," he said, turning to her. "I still can't understand how you could just leave them the way you did. I don't understand how you could not bother to contact your own daughter at least," his voice gained energy with the momentum, "and I certainly don't understand why you suddenly want to come back and expect that it will be all right that you do."

This time Kate turned away.

"You hate me."

Part of him wanted to say, yes. But it wouldn't be true. He had never hated her.

"No," he said instead, his voice softening a little, "I just don't understand you."

Her whole body turned to him in an effort to lend her words more weight.

"I thought that you, above all others would, you know. Surely *you* could understand that when you are called to the Spirit ..."

Her phrasing irked him, particularly now.

"But you gave up your family!"

She looked at him coolly. Silence filled the car.

"Why have you really come back, Kate?"

"To look after my daughter." There was something malicious in her tone. "And, by the way, my name's *Kat*!"

Silence again. Rupert started the car and they headed out into the busy morning traffic to home. Whose home? He thought.

"We need to talk about Neti," he said, not looking at her. He felt like everything about him was prickling in her presence.

"How does she feel about me coming home?" Kat said. She spoke quietly now and there was a slight tremor in her voice.

"She's excited." He wished he could have put it in a way that would provoke the most guilt. "Oh?" she said with more energy.

"But she's very confused," Rupert added quickly, "and I am very worried about her."

"So am I Ru." Kat hesitated. "What is she like?"

The question bothered him and accentuated the distance between mother and daughter. He suspected that she felt it too.

"Vulnerable."

Kat looked at him with a pained expression. He wasn't looking at her as he drove, but he could feel it. He sighed.

"She's fifteen, as you know. Physically, she's a lot like Ross when he was young ... especially since she's cut her hair."

He smiled to himself when he thought of Ross and Neti. It dawned on him that, of course, she must resemble himself, too.

"But she has some of your features ... around the eyes and chin I think." He looked again at Kat to assess the truth of this statement. Yes, he thought, she is like her mother.

"Under normal circumstances, Neti is lively but soft-hearted. She's also very intelligent." Rupert wondered what circumstances in his niece's life had ever been normal. "However, over the last month she has become increasingly moody and unhappy, which is understandable."

"How did she take her father's death?"

"She hasn't spoken of him. I'm worried about that."

Rupert thought that he could hear Kat's brain ticking over.

"They were very close, *very* close. He was a devoted father." He knew that he was labouring the point, but he suddenly felt the need to defend his brother to this woman. Talking to her now, he felt that he was betraying Ross.

"I would never have expected him to be anything less." Kat spoke forcefully, seeming to know that her credibility as Neti's mother was at stake. "I've always thought about her, Ru, I just didn't want to interfere. I know that I hurt Ross, but I suppose I hoped that he would remarry and that Neti would have a woman she could talk to. I didn't feel that I had a right to her anymore."

"And now?" Rupert was amazed at how she could make herself seem almost noble. What bothered him more was that he was almost accepting her excuses.

Kat paused before answering, "Well, he didn't remarry ... and now he's dead and Neti has no-one."

It was like a stab at his heart.

"She has me."

He turned into their street.

"Oh, Ru, I'm sorry. I am so very grateful that you were willing to take care of Neti. You couldn't have made that decision easily. But what a sacrifice! I hope she appreciates what you were willing to do for her ... I'll make sure that she does—"

"*I just want you to take care of her, Kate,*" he cut across her rambling, feeling like he was going to snap at any moment. "Don't let her down. *Please!*"

He pulled into the driveway and jerked to a halt.

"She needs your attention," he said facing her. "She needs to come first! Are you capable of that?"

Kat was staring at the house of her past life, almost ignoring him. In complete exasperation he hit the steering wheel and got out of the car. She did not move.

Rupert held the door open for her. She rallied and climbed out of the car, her movements suggesting that she had aged in just a few minutes. He bent to assist her, but she handed him her bag instead.

———

He went ahead and opened the front door. As Kat cast a wary eye around her, she felt overwhelmed with déjà vu — little had changed. The lawn was neatly mown, but courageous flowers struggled through the tangle of weeds in the beds. There was evidence though of someone's attempt to bring order into the garden — cleared spots in the beds where newly planted seedlings tried to take root. She knew that it would be Rupert, always so tidy and tight. He would not, could not, understand anarchy.

She dreaded stepping through the door, but he held it open for her. Her breath came faster and made her feel weak and light-headed. She focused on her mantra, repeating it over and over to herself. She stood inside the door and looked around her — nothing had changed. *Nothing*.

"Are you alright?"

His voice startled her, and she spun around to him, causing her to feel giddy. He dropped her bag on the floor and escorted her to the couch.

"Can I get you something?"

He sounded genuinely concerned.

"I'll be all right." She rummaged in the handbag still hanging from her shoulder. "I'm okay, Ru. Just a long trip. A glass of water?"

"Of course," he said, heading to the kitchen immediately.

Kat unzipped her bag hurriedly and rummaged for a moment. She popped two pills into her mouth just as he returned. He hadn't seen.

"Thanks," she said, having already swallowed them. She took a sip from the glass and placed it on the coffee table.

"So ... Here I am," she said, her arms thrown out in a gesture to the house.

Rupert was still standing. He took her bag and placed it in Ross's bedroom.

"I have to go back to work, K ... Kat, for just a couple of hours. I'll pick Neti up on the way home. Will you be all right on your own?"

"Oh. Yes." She was disturbed by this information. She thought for a moment and then said, "Ru, don't move out just yet. Neti and I will need some time to get to know each other. It might be better if you're here to break the ice for a while."

"If you're sure that's what you want."

"Yes," she said quickly.

"I'll see you in a few hours then ... with Neti."

"Fine." She felt uncertain. "Can I do anything for dinner?" she called after him as he headed out the door.

"I'll bring something home with me," he called back. "See you then."

"Okay ..." Her voice was timid. "See you then."

Kat trembled where she sat, the ghosts of her past rushing at her as soon as the door closed behind him.

Kat was starting to think that she had made a terrible mistake. Throughout the long journey from Byron Bay, she had tried to convince herself that she was doing the right thing. But as the train had approached Southern Cross Station, and when she had seen Rupert standing there passively by the gate, she knew that she hadn't.

She told herself that she was just tired, that she felt nauseous from the train, that it was the grey weather of a Melbourne autumn day. She thought that when she stepped off the train, by hurrying to Rupert, she would outrun her doubts. If only he had smiled, greeted her warmly, she might have won.

Kat didn't know why she should expect anything else from him. The way in which she had left Ross and Neti was wrong, she knew that and had lived with the guilt of it. So often over the last ten years, she had wanted to contact Neti, but could not face Ross and the pain she had caused him. When Rupert wrote of Ross's death, a way opened for her to reconcile with her daughter. It had seemed so hopeful, and right when Kat was in Byron Bay, and she knew she had to leave there too. But now, faced with the reality of the life she had left behind ten years ago, nothing seemed right.

She closed her eyes and allowed the pills to take effect.

CHAPTER FIVE

Once again, Rupert found himself eating on his own. For the first few nights, following Kat's return, the three of them sat, a motley crew around the table — an anxious Rupert, a sedated Kat and Neti, who was able to deliver both bonhomie to her mother and a vicious patronising of her uncle in the one breath. None of them could sustain it for long.

Rupert marvelled at the speed at which Neti adjusted to the presence of the mother she had never really known, the woman who had abandoned her.

The day Kat had returned, Rupert had fretted so much about the reunion between mother and daughter that he felt physically ill. When he had waited for Neti outside the school, he was shaking. She had run to the car, slammed the door quickly behind her and sat with her body leaning forward, barely acknowledging him. Is she home? she had said, looking at him from the corner of her eye. Yes, he had answered through a cough. When they pulled up in the driveway, he heard her sharp intake of breath. He took the opportunity to speak before they went inside.

"Neti ... If it gets too hard for you, please tell me ... We'll work something out."

He heard her scoff and saw that she was picking at a loose thread on the cuff of her jumper, and he suspected that her jaw was clenched. She did not rush to open the car door but kept tugging at the thread and winding it about her finger. Rupert was saddened as he watched her. Neti's similarity to Ross seemed so pronounced at this moment, and he was over-whelmed with the sense of betraying his brother. He wished he could back the car out of the drive and keep going, anywhere, taking Neti away from the emotional nightmare that he was certain they would all face.

Rupert had envisaged Kat waiting at the door when they arrived. She wasn't there. Neti seemed unsure what to do when they stepped inside an apparently empty house. She looked up at him uncertainly. He felt a surge of panic. Surely not now ... He scanned the lounge room for a sign of Kat's presence. Her handbag was still by the chair where he had left her earlier, the contents half spilled onto the floor. The curtains had been drawn together haphazardly.

"Put your bag in your room, Neti," he said, handing it to her. Adopting a cheering tone, he added, "Kate mustn't have heard us come in." With dread, he began to search the house, beginning with Ross's room where Kat was to stay ... to live. Her luggage was where he had left it, but she was not there. Nor was she in the kitchen, but she had been — there were spilt coffee grains and drops of milk on the bench. He could see that the door to the spare room in which he slept was ajar. When he looked in, he saw Kat lying on the bed with her back to him; a coffee cup sat precariously on the bedside table. Tentatively, he walked around the bed. She was not asleep as he had first thought but was staring vacantly out the window. The glazed look in her eyes startled him and, for a moment, he felt a rush of fear.

"Kate ..."

Without moving her head, her eyes shifted slowly to his.

"Are you alright?" he said.

"I can't ... I can't ..." she said quietly, her eyes having left his to return to the window.

Rupert sat down on the edge of the bed. She reached out suddenly and gripped his hand.

"Ru?"

There was a pleading in her voice. He thought of Neti. She would be waiting. He shook his hand free of her.

"Kate!" He gripped her arm and bent towards her so she could hear the urgency in his voice, "*Neti is out there! She's waiting for you!*"

Kat propped herself up and looked dazed, but at least responded to him.

"I can't Ru ... Oh ... What have I done?"

An unfamiliar anger rose in Rupert. His head pounded. He wanted to shake her ... *hit* her. He recoiled from the emotion. He was also aware that this was an opportunity for Kat to leave their lives. But it was too late now.

"*Please, Kate.*" He was pleading with her. "*For Neti's sake, please get up and greet her!*"

Kat sat up straighter. She smoothed her hair from her face and casually reached for the coffee cup. She took a sip. "It's Kat. Remember?" she said surprisingly evenly and looking him in the eye. "Don't worry Rupert. I'm ready to play Mum."

Rupert was caught off-guard by the changed tone of her voice. He stood up. Kat leaned back against the bedhead and took another sip from the cup. Rupert hesitated as he left the room.

"I'll be out in a minute," she said calmly.

Neti was standing in the lounge room with her back to him. Her arms dangled awkwardly by her side and her posture was stiffened. She had changed from her school uniform into a pair of jeans and a hooded windcheater. From the back view she could have been mistaken for a boy.

"Neti." Rupert approached carefully so as not to startle her. She turned to him. "Just as I'd thought," once again adding a cheerful lilt to his voice, "Kat was exhausted from the trip and dozed off! She couldn't believe the time when I woke her!" Rupert scanned Neti's face for a sign that she did not believe him. "She'll be out in a moment."

Neti's eyes were wide, and her mouth was rounded as if to make a soft exclamation. She looked past him and, when Rupert saw the jerk of her jaw and the fleeting look of panic in her eyes, he knew that Kat was behind him. He was caught in the tension between them.

"*Oh ... look at you!*"

Rupert heard Kat's exclamation behind him and could feel her moving forward. He was still watching Neti who had now taken a tiny step back at the same time raising one hand to her hip. She stood self-consciously and the hand, which Rupert could see was trembling, slipped from her hip to her side.

He could stop it now, he thought. He was in a physical position to bar Kat's way. Once she stepped past him the opportunity would be lost. It was too late. Kat rushed past him and wrapped the startled Neti in her arms.

"*My poor darling!*" Kat cried into Neti's ear.

Looking over Kat's shoulder, Neti sought reassurance in Rupert's face.

He smiled. He had betrayed her, and he smiled.

Neti turned and rested her head in the crook of her mother's neck. The hair on the back of Kat's head was unbrushed and knotted from sleep. Rupert saw that Neti, waif-thin, was already as tall as her mother who stood in stockinged feet. He looked away.

"My baby, my baby," Kat cooed and stroked Neti's hair.

Releasing Neti, Kat held her at arm's length. "How beautiful you are!" she said, running her hand through Neti's spiked hair and tracing the shape of her face with a finger. Neti, already it seemed to Rupert, was looking adoringly at her mother. Rupert's moment, his opportunity and, now, his purpose here, were over.

Leaving the two of them, he went to the kitchen to prepare dinner, leaving the door ajar in case Neti needed him. He could not hear what they were saying to each other, but the constant murmur of the two voices should have reassured him that all was well. Instead, he was filled with apprehension and, if he admitted it to himself, envy.

Dinner that night was a highly-strung affair, or so it seemed to Rupert. For the most part, Kat and Neti were locked in each other's company, with occasional questions from Kat directed to him. Throughout he kept a close eye on Neti. Her eyes never left her mother.

Despite her earlier disposition in the bedroom, Kat seemed remarkably composed, speaking to Neti in calm, measured tones, asking questions of her daughter with what seemed to be sincere interest. Neti, for her part, seemed to have mellowed in the presence of her mother and seemed, to Rupert, to be more child-like and innocent than he had seen her since her father's death. He wondered, as he watched them, if he had been wrong about Kat, that perhaps her behaviour earlier in the bedroom was an aberration, brought on by fatigue and the anxiety he was certain this meeting must have held for her. He felt a small, fleeting comfort in this thought until he caught Kat watching him; she wore a look of victory.

After dinner, Rupert offered to clean up while Neti took

Kat into her bedroom. Neti had wanted to show her mother her collections. When he had finished, he did his routine inspection of the pantry for the weekly shopping. He realized, as he made his list, that this simple routine that he had come to enjoy would probably now be taken over by Kat.

He waited for Kat and Neti in the lounge room. They had been in there for a long time and, even with the bedroom door closed, Rupert could hear them laughing — Kat raucously at times. He knocked on the door. They were laughing and didn't hear him. When he looked in, mother and daughter were sitting cross-legged on the floor playing a game of cards. Kat looked up at him.

"Rupert! Come in and join us!" She shifted her position to make room for him. Neti looked at him darkly.

"No, I've just come to say that I'm going to my room ... to read. Is there anything I can get you before I go?"

Kat's expression changed to one of panic.

"Rupert..." She got up stiffly. She turned to Neti, "I'll be back in a minute darling," she said brightly. The moment she turned back to Rupert her expression changed again. "Can I speak to you?" She ushered him through the doorway. "Ru," she whispered, pulling the door closed behind her. "Where am I to sleep?"

He was puzzled by her question, but she went on quickly.

"I *can't* sleep in that room!" She gestured with her head to Ross's room, the room she had shared with him many years before. "Please Ru ... Let me sleep in the spare room?"

Rupert understood her concern. He didn't want to sleep there either, for the same and for vastly different reasons from Kat. He also did not want *her* to sleep in his brother's bed.

The day before, Rupert had had to face the room, to prepare it for her. Strangely, it had not been Ross's clothes that had distressed him as he folded them into bags. It was when he pulled back the bedcover to change the sheets that his heart sank. Though clean, one side of the fitted sheet was worn — not threadbare, indicating Ross's favourite side of the bed.

"I think you should ..." he finally answered her.

"*No! Ru.*" Kat's eyes were wild.

Rupert faltered for a moment, but went on firmly, "It would be important to Neti that you're close by." And, he thought, to fill the void in that room.

Kat's expression hardened. "You're not going to make this any easier on me, are you?"

Rupert answered her quickly, "This isn't about me or you, Kat. Neti is our priority. I'm not enamoured with the idea of your return. I admit that. But Neti wants you here and, as her mother, you could do more for her than I could probably ever do."

"You don't think I'm capable of it. Do you Rupert?" Kat's eyes narrowed.

"No," he said without hesitation. "But I sincerely hope that I'm wrong."

With that, he left Kat standing at Neti's door, unwilling to discuss it further. Kat knew what she was coming back to, he consoled himself, and she must accept that.

That first night following Kat's return, Rupert's sleep came in infrequent fits, despite the emotional drain of the day. Kat's behaviour caused him concern. In his memory of her she had always been excitable, living life largely and furiously. Although he knew her highs, he did not recollect the lows, although, as her brother-in-law, he might not have been privy to them. Ross had never mentioned them, but then, he was so accepting of others, including their faults, that he may have thought little of it. Although it was apparent that there were difficulties between them in the years after Neti's birth, Kat had seemed more restless, more critical and more dynamic than before it. Her sudden departure was typical of her impetuous nature and, as a result, Ross never quite came to terms with the fact that she was not coming home.

This older Kat was subdued, as if life had been leaking out of her for the last ten years. The incident in the bedroom had revealed to Rupert a side of her he had never seen, nor thought he would ever see — a vulnerable woman.

She loves me, Neti thought, watching her mother on the couch out of the corner of her eye, although it had taken her a little while to allow herself to believe it. Neti remembered when she first saw her mother coming into the room behind Rupert. She remembered, too, that she had been very nervous, excited though, but tongue-tied as well. Kat had hugged her, and Rupert had smiled with approval. No doubt, Neti thought, he couldn't wait to hand her over and go back to his weird, real life.

Straight away Neti had liked Kat, and they had sat on the floor of her bedroom that first night and talked and played cards like ... sisters. She tried to imagine Polly doing the same with her mother. *No way!* she thought with a laugh and a small sense of pride.

When Kat drove her to school, Neti lingered, making up things to talk about, to keep her mother there long enough so that other latecomers could see her. *So* much better than being dropped off early by her boring uncle. She'd wanted to get away quickly on those mornings, in case someone saw him.

The other reason, she knew, was that people were shocked to see him, and there had been a rumour at school that Neti had made up a story about her father's death. Miss Lees had sent her out of assembly on an errand, and Polly told Neti that Miss Lees had put an end to the rumours then.

Neti contracted the thought until it was squeezed from her mind.

Now, it seemed that every day was like a holiday. Kat was fun. She was a 'free spirit', Neti thought, and she applied this principle to her daughter. If Neti didn't want to do her homework, that was okay by her, and it wasn't too hard to tell that Kat held contempt for anything resembling an institution. Neti liked this freedom and felt that she was, perhaps, more like her mother than she had thought. But Rupert was becoming a pain. Adopting a new policy for herself, Neti had decided that her Geography assignment could wait. He had remembered when it was due as he'd helped her collect information for it. Neti was aware of the tension that this created between her mother and her uncle, but in the end, Kat gave in.

"Just do it, love," she'd said to Neti with a tired voice.

Neti couldn't wait until Rupert was gone.

She looked across to the dining area and could see his lone figure sitting at the table eating his meal. Part of her felt that she should go to him and say something kind. Instead, she picked up a cushion lying next to her on the couch and threw it at Kat. For a moment, she thought she saw a look of annoyance on her mother's face, but Kat returned the cushion with equal force. They both laughed and settled to watch the television.

Kat's cool, Neti thought with pride.

Rupert laboured through the next few days and nights, feeling as though he had been recast into a role for which he had not prepared.

Since that first day, Kat seemed relatively composed, albeit subdued, and had moved reluctantly into Ross's bedroom. She was the last to bed of a night, often sitting in the silence of the lounge room for hours, and when she finally did go to bed, Rupert would hear her get up several times. In the morning, she would wake just in time to drive Neti to school, her eyes puffy and red-rimmed. But she greeted her daughter cheerfully despite the strain of being up so early.

Kat tried, in those first few days, to endorse the routine that Rupert had established for Neti, including eating meals at the table. The tension that existed between them, the averted eyes and stilted talk, became too much for her and she took to eating in front of the television. Neti followed.

Rupert now ate alone, while Neti and Kat, feet curled under them, ate theirs on their laps, engrossing themselves in the lives of the characters from *Summer Bay*. He was not able to get close to Neti now and could only guess, from the way she sauntered around the house, that she was beginning to adopt her new role as Kat's daughter with great relish. On one occasion, however, Neti brought out her camera and, setting it up on the table, took a photograph of the three of them. This incident left Rupert somewhat bewildered, as most of the time she ignored him. If he had ever had significance in Neti's life, he seemed to be redundant now. There was little left to mark his influence — even at the most basic level. Not only were meals together abandoned, so too was the homework routine. Kat seemed to be oblivious, if not antagonistic, to the need for order.

His feeling of impotence was heightened by the lack of structure in his day. Rupert had never known a time in his adult years when he was not busy with work, study or both, and now, he found himself lying on his bed in the middle of the day overcome by a feeling of lethargy.

Kat was there on those days — lying on her bed or, more

often, on Neti's while she was at school. On these days, the air prickled between them. Rupert felt the need to speak with her but couldn't muster the courage. Kat sensed it and so they skirted each other to avoid unwanted conversation.

The longer he had to himself, however, the more time Rupert had to think about Kat, and Ross, and the pain her leaving had caused his brother. Did she know what she had done? Did she know his brother mourned her for ten years, that his hope had eroded, and his sorrow had turned to bitterness? How, despite his inability to come to terms with it, along with his attempts to drown it, he never missed a day's work; he never failed his daughter in any way that a child would recognize.

As Rupert thought these things, the lethargy turned to frustration. Lying on his bed, he heard Kat move about in the kitchen. It was time to talk.

Kat was heading for the telephone when Rupert came into the kitchen. She faltered when she saw him and steered away from it. Despite the cool of the morning, Rupert noticed her feet were bare except for the ring she wore on one toe.

"Kat," Rupert said to her half-turned back.

She turned to him guiltily. "Morning Ru. You startled me. I thought you'd gone out."

Rupert moved towards the kettle. "Cup of tea?"

"No ... I don't think so." Kat seemed to sense his intention to talk and became agitated. She made moves to leave the kitchen.

"We need to talk, Kat," Rupert said.

"About?" She smiled innocently, but her eyes were furtive.

"So much," he said, "what's gone before and where we're going now."

She raised her eyebrows at the inevitability of the conversation.

"Why did you go?"

Rupert felt as if a valve was releasing as he finally asked this ten-year-old question. Kat's expression remained impassive.

"Straight to the heart of it, eh Ru?" She sighed. "What can I tell you now, after all these years? It was over — I didn't love Ross anymore."

"But you had a child!" Despite Rupert's intention to remain calm, Kat's almost flippant answer enraged him. He breathed deeply. "Marriages break down, Kat. But you abandoned them. There was no warning, no explanation."

"Life is not as cut-and-dry as you have tried to live it. I had my reasons, not least the fact that I knew, at the time, that I was incapable of raising a child."

"Pity you didn't think about that beforehand." Rupert felt a ripple of shame as he said it, but Kat merely nodded with the predictability of it.

"*So* righteous you are, Rupert. You've never really known what it means to live and to struggle, have you?"

"I've known pain," he said.

"What have you known?" Her voice sounded shrill. "You ran from it, remember? I could ask *you* to explain! Why did you abandon your brother, your mother and ... " she hesitated, "is your father still alive, Ru?"

Rupert was silent.

"Who visits him now? Now that Ross has gone?"

Rupert had expected a backlash but was not prepared for this. He was at a loss to answer her.

"Not you, I'll bet." Kat's voice sounded triumphant. Rupert's silence provided her with the opportunity to let all guns fire, or to walk away.

"Do you?" she pressed him, but her voice was softer now.

"No, I don't see him," Rupert answered her with a mixture of defiance and shame.

"Ru." Kat moved towards him and touched him gently on

the arm. "You *must* see him — before it's too late. You'll regret it if you don't."

"I doubt that."

"There's something I don't understand," Kat said softly, "why do you find it so hard to forgive?"

Rupert did not answer her but turned his back and went to his room, closing the door quietly behind him.

CHAPTER SIX

"Athena?"

"Rupert." Athena was surprised to hear the voice at the other end of the telephone. "How are you?"

"Well ... I think."

She heard the smile in his voice.

"I don't know if you remember," he continued, "but I know I owe you a meal."

He sounded nervous, Athena thought, and at the same time, she wondered how often he might have asked a woman out. She replied quickly and reassuringly, "I do recall you mentioning something of the kind."

"Good ... good."

She waited. After a pause, he continued.

"Dinner? Would dinner suit you?"

"That would be nice. When do you mean?"

"Tonight?"

"Oh!" Athena was surprised but tried not to show it, "At your home? And with your niece ... Neti?"

Rupert told her briefly about the change in his circumstances brought about by the return of Neti's mother. Athena could hear the strain in his voice as he relayed this news and decided to take control of the dinner invitation.

"Do you like Thai, Rupert? I know a very nice restaurant." She proceeded to make the arrangements for the evening. Though she was somewhat bemused by this man, she smiled to herself when she put down the receiver.

Rupert scrutinised himself in the long mirror. He was suddenly conscious of how tired his clothes looked — or was it him? Maybe it was both. Nothing looked right. He must have lost weight, he mused, because he felt he resembled a flagpole draped in an oversized and tatty flag. He needed a haircut too: his wiry curls, normally cut short and carefully groomed, refused to comply with the comb. He looked at his face. Strange, what time will do, he thought. His features still seemed hawkish though, as they had done when he was in his teens. He tried to remember a nickname given to him by a girl he had been smitten with at fourteen. "Eagle-beak", he recalled.

He was nervous about this evening. He tried to rationalise it. He had been out to dinner before — with a woman. Marjorie and he had gone out frequently for a meal together in their early years. What was different? He had been anxious when he rang Athena, worrying that he was being presumptuous, or that she might think that he was being too forward, but she had reacted matter-of-factly enough. He was making too much of it himself. He was being silly ... yes, that's how he felt he looked ... silly.

Rupert wondered now why he had called Athena. He had been lying on his bed, once again, following his conversation

83

with Kat. He was tired of the sight of the ceiling now, tired of the feeling of inadequacy and uselessness. He tried to pray. He said the words, and spoke them as if by saying them aloud their meaning would be clear to him, but they rang hollow in his ears. He tried to force himself to believe and recognized the futility of that. He lay motionless and thoughtless, waiting for grace to be given to him in his time of need. He was met with mocking silence that offered no intimacy. He thought of the day-to-day of his life, but there was little to comfort him there. He thought of Athena and while he retained that thought, of her, he felt better. He rang her.

Rupert took another look at himself in the mirror and decided that nothing could be done about the look of the lean and ageing man facing him. He picked up his car keys. Kat seemed to be hovering in the lounge room, waiting for him as he prepared to leave.

"Let me have a look at you," she said moving toward him.

He stepped back noticing that her face looked flushed, and her eyes glazed.

"Come on, Ru ..." she said following him, "I've never seen you dressed for a date before."

"It's not a date, Kat," he said with irritation.

She ignored him. "Surely you could have found something better to wear than that!"

At that moment, Neti appeared on her way to the kitchen.

"Look at Ru, Neti, love. He's going on a date." She laughed aloud.

Neti looked at her mother and to Rupert in bewilderment. She hesitated and Rupert didn't know if he imagined a look of disappointment in her face.

"Kat, *please*," Rupert said, exasperated with her now. "I'm just going out for dinner with a friend," he said to Neti, feeling the need to explain himself.

"Whatever," she said shrugging her shoulders and continued to the kitchen.

"Have a good time, Ru," Kat called mockingly as he was leaving. "Don't do anything I wouldn't do!" she added to his back before the door closed.

As Athena was working until late, they had decided to meet at the restaurant she had suggested. She was there when he arrived and watched him as he came in. He waved when he saw her and self-consciously manoeuvred his way between the tables. He looked different, she thought, his hair longer and his overall appearance less meticulously groomed. She liked his way, though — simple clothing and no adornments. She smiled at her own contradiction; she liked to buy good quality, and that usually meant more expensive clothing.

"Hello, Rupert," she said smiling up at him.

"Hello," he said, smiling too as he sat, then looking around him, "this is nice."

They talked awkwardly at first, beginning with pleasantries, but the conversation eventually found its way to Rupert's circumstances at home. Athena was surprised to hear that Neti's mother had returned. At first, she thought that this would be a good thing, perhaps relieving Rupert of a responsibility that was too much for him, however, although Rupert did not denigrate his sister-in-law, Athena could not fail to see that he was far from happy to see her home.

"How old is Neti did you say?"

"Fifteen."

"That's my brother Toby's age."

Over two courses of exotic fare that Athena noticed Rupert ate with quiet enthusiasm, she told him about her brother, Toby, who had Down syndrome, and who preferred to be known as 'Tobias', with only those within the family granted permission to call him Toby. She spoke of her family — of how her mother was a writer and her father an artist; that she was born when her parents were young and struggling to achieve some recognition in their respective arts; of how she travelled the world with them in her young years and spent several of those in Italy where she became fluent in Italian. The family returned to Australia when Athena was thirteen. By then, both parents had paved a way in their careers and were homesick for the country of their birth. They settled on a property on the Mornington Peninsula where they still lived and worked. When Athena's parents were in their forties, and she was eighteen, Toby was born.

"He's the light of our lives," said Athena, her eyes bright with the thought of her brother. "Although I live in town, I have Toby with me a couple of nights a week while he attends a special school. I love to have him with me, and it helps to give my parents a break too."

Rupert listened attentively, smiling all the while. "You live alone then? Other than when Toby comes?"

Athena laughed. "Yes. I don't have time for a relationship if that's what you mean!" She continued more seriously, "I did have a relationship once. We were going to get married but ... I don't know, life, and I suppose Toby got in the way of us. He is a commitment, my brother, but I wouldn't have it any other way." She stopped for a moment. She hadn't thought about Mark for quite a while, burying herself in her work and her brother. It surprised her now how little of the pain remained.

"What about you, Rupert? What do you think you'll do now?"

He seemed to be considering her question. "Do you know, for the first time in twenty-five years, I have no idea."

Athena nodded. "It's hard," she said, "the point it sounds

like you've reached. That point when we lose the map and can't entrust the way to memory because we suspect the destination has changed too."

He paused before speaking.

"I'm not certain that I knew what my destination was before. I don't think I gave it a lot of thought actually."

She studied him closely.

"Perhaps you were happy just being Rupert Brown."

"Hmm," he said smiling, "we seem to be getting back to me again."

"Well, Rupert Brown, could I offer you a new destination?"

He looked at her quizzically, which made her laugh.

"My place for a cup of tea ... or coffee?" she said in explanation.

He took his time in answering and seemed to be taking her in. Athena blushed.

"That's the clearest direction I've had in a while," he said in acceptance of her invitation.

———

Rupert followed Athena's car to her single-fronted home, which he was surprised to see was only a few blocks from where he lived. Inside, the house was deceptively spacious and modern. Athena directed him to the seating end of the open-plan room that served as her kitchen, lounge-room and, by the look of the book-lined wall and desk, her study.

"Make yourself at home, Rupert," Athena called to him from the kitchen end of the room while she put the kettle on, "I won't be a moment," she added, heading out of the room.

He was drawn to the bookcase and scanned the titles there. Largely, the books were science texts, but he noticed a smattering of philosophical works by Nietzsche and, he noticed with interest, Thomas Aquinas. He took the latter from the shelf and was leafing through the pages when Athena returned. She had changed from her daywear of skirt and jumper to a woollen tracksuit and comfortable shoes.

"What did you find?" she said, noticing the book in Rupert's hand.

"Aquinas. I'm surprised," he said, turning the cover towards her.

"Really? Why is that?" she called over her shoulder as she went to turn off the whistling kettle. "He was a fine philosopher."

"I don't know ... I just didn't think that ..." Rupert's voice trailed off as he thought about it. "I suppose I expected to find Descartes."

"Oh, he's there too!" Athena said with a laugh as she prepared the tea.

Rupert considered the two philosophers — Descartes and his mind/body dualism and influence on the ultimate separation of science and religion, and Aquinas before him, confident that the natural world was a reflection of the law of God. He wondered where Athena sat in relation to these two views in her work in neuroscience and consciousness. Before he could ask the question, she answered him, carrying a tray with tea to the table between the settees.

"I still don't know where I sit with them. Probably more with Descartes as I have trouble with the 'god' angle of Aquinas, as you know. But there is some really interesting research going on in my field." She went to her desk and found an article that she offered him. "You might be interested in this," she said, pointing to a particular passage.

Rupert took it and sat on the settee while Athena sat next to him pouring the tea. He read the passage, "Results of study done at the University of Pennsylvania on the brain function of people engaged in Tibetan meditation indicate that the brain's amygdala, which translates sensory impressions into emotions, somehow generates a sense of religious awe. Whether these experiences of religious awe are 'real' or just the brain's way of helping us deal with sad realities is yet to be answered ..."

"Yes, *helping us deal with sad realities*," Rupert quoted aloud. "This is interesting." He gave it back to Athena. "Is this university leading in the research?"

"Yes," she said, "as a matter of fact, I have been offered a bursary to continue my own research there."

"That's wonderful for you," he said but didn't sound as pleased as he should have. "Will you go?"

"It's an offer too good to refuse, but there is a lot to consider, not the least my brother, Toby. I need to make up my mind by the end of the month ... just three weeks."

Rupert was quiet and lost in thought. Athena offered him a biscuit, but she too was quiet.

"Care to see some photographs?" she said finally. "Say no if you want to — they can be a real bore when you don't know anyone in them."

Rupert was pleased to see them. The album was on the coffee table in front of them. She lifted it to her lap and kicked off her shoes, curling her legs under her. This caused her to lean on him and she needed to readjust herself several times.

For the next hour, they went through the photographs one by one, and Rupert had a much clearer image of her family and her life as a result. Athena was obviously very close to, not only her parents and brother Toby, but her extended family and network of friends. He smiled at the way she would talk about this person and that, relating anecdotal stories about them with affection and breaking off into a related thought. Several times, she would stop and check that he wasn't bored. He wasn't. In fact, he had not felt this relaxed and comfortable for a very long time.

He could have sat with her for much longer, but when he checked his watch, he was surprised at how late it was.

"I must go," he said regretfully, when they had finished the album and there was a lull in conversation.

She didn't say anything but stood up with him.

"Thanks for this evening. I really enjoyed myself," he said and meant it.

"So did I. And thank you for the dinner, although you really didn't have to do that."

She walked him to the door.

"Well," they said together laughing and said their goodbyes.

He walked down the path, but before she had closed the door, he called spontaneously, "Is it all right if I call you again, soon?"

"Yes," she called back smiling. "Yes, I'd like that."

As Rupert had anticipated, Kat was still awake when he got home, sitting in front of the television. Although Neti had developed the habit of sitting up with her mother until much later than her usual time, tonight she was in bed.

"Have fun did you, Ru?" Kat said in a facetious tone.

The contrast of his life in this house with the evening he had just spent with Athena struck him harshly. The energy he had gained in Athena's presence was sapped from him instantly in Kat's. Her question did not deserve an answer and he walked past her to his room.

"Harder than you thought, eh? Operating in the real world?" she called after him, but he closed the door before she could finish.

. . .

That night, Rupert slept soundly. In the early morning, he dreamed of holding Athena's hand. He woke up, groggy with the depth and the emotion of the dream and lay awake for some time trying to come to grips with what it could mean.

The following day he spent quietly, his mind alternating between not wanting to think about Athena and the dream and wanting to surrender to the bliss of it.

Neti had left, to spend a few days of the school holidays with her friend, Polly, and her family. Rupert was pleased — Polly was a good influence on Neti, and he felt that it would do her good. Neti had not wanted to go at first, being still wrapped in her mother's presence, but surprisingly, Kat encouraged her to. Rupert didn't relish the thought of spending these days with Kat but thought that it could provide an opportunity to iron out their differences and to establish a more solid basis on which to build a home for Neti. He was conscious too, that he was probably assigning himself a role in Kat and Neti's lives that would not be offered.

He busied himself cleaning the house — a task Kat seemed more than willing to leave to him while she embroidered more coloured thread into an intricately designed tapestry. In a cynical moment, Rupert wondered if she ever sewed in a conflicting thread.

He was cleaning the bathroom when he heard a knock at the front door, and Kat answered it. He could hear two voices as Kat and the visitor moved to the lounge room. Kat came to look for him.

"Ru," she said, finding him bent over the bath. "You have a visitor."

There was a tone in her voice that made him look up quickly.

"Who is it?"

"Your lady-friend, I'd say."

Rupert could feel himself blush.

"Marjorie," Kat added, relishing the moment.

Rupert wondered if his fleeting disappointment showed but was surprised and pleased to learn that it was Marjorie.

"Marjorie is an old friend and my colleague." He was irritated but felt a small pleasure in Kat's mistake.

This news did not seem to dispel Kat's misconception. She prepared to retort, but Rupert walked past her, leaving her to voice it to the bathroom mirror.

Marjorie greeted her friend warmly and was scanning his face as if to determine his emotional and physical state. Her brow furrowed.

They sat together on the couch.

"Are you alright?" she said, placing a hand on his shoulder.

He nodded in reassurance.

"I have news, of Matthew," Marjorie said with a note of regret in her voice.

Rupert was startled at the mention of his dear friend's name. He shared a deep and abiding friendship with his mentor, Matthew, who had been the catalyst for Rupert's conversion to Catholicism.

"Matthew? What's wrong?"

"The Community has rung, looking for you, Rupert. Matthew is ailing, but he has been asking for you, that is, asking for 'Elijah'. They suspected that this was his name for you. I remembered that you had told me."

"How long?" Rupert said, staring ahead of him.

When Rupert had last seen Matthew, only a month previously, he was displaying some symptoms of dementia, but was otherwise well and in good spirits.

"He came down with a viral infection a month ago — it's turned to pneumonia".

As the reality of Matthew's condition sank in, Rupert could feel the return of an all too familiar despair that edged his mind into its protective void.

"I'll leave tomorrow," he said, as much to himself as to Marjorie.

Marjorie stayed on for a while, talking with Rupert about anecdotal happenings in the faculty, but all the time keeping an eye on him. This news, so quickly on the heels of Ross's death, could only compound the grief that Rupert was already experiencing.

"Do you know," Rupert said to her, "since Ross has died, with everything that has happened ... I have barely given Matthew a thought."

"You couldn't possibly have known!" Marjorie responded to the sound of guilt in his voice. "Matthew has had a long life, Rupert," she added, trying to encourage a more positive perspective.

He smiled and looked down at his hands, but a shadow crossed his face.

"Would you like me to come with you tomorrow?" Marjorie offered.

Rupert shook his head.

When Marjorie had left, Rupert sat for a while longer in the lounge room. Mercifully, Kat had kept her distance while Marjorie had been there, but she now appeared from her room. If she had planned to follow her earlier theme, she thought better of it, seeing Rupert sitting silently in the day's twilight. She began to move towards him, but seemed to change her mind and, instead, picked up the needlework that she had left on the floor earlier and retreated to her room.

Rupert sat for a long time. Eventually, he found his way

from the mire of his thoughts to an awareness of the present and the cold and dark of the room. He rallied himself and, though feeling groggy, he left the house. He drove for some time, grateful for the distraction it provided and the strangely comforting hum of the engine beneath him.

After some time, he found himself driving down Athena's street. When he saw her house, he felt an urgency to see her, but remembering his dream, he could no longer ascertain what his motives might be. He parked the car in the street while he debated them. Though part of him was reluctant to knock on her door, a bolder part did not hesitate.

Athena answered his knock with a look of surprise.

"Come in," she invited him warmly and, much to Rupert's relief, did not question as to why he had come. "You can meet Toby."

As they entered the large room, Rupert could see the back of a boy's ruffled hair on the settee.

"Tobe," Athena called to him, "I want you to meet someone."

Without hesitation, the boy abandoned what he was doing and ran to his sister. Once in the safety of Athena's arms, he turned his head into her, occasionally peeking a look at the stranger. At fifteen, Toby was the size of a ten-year-old and Rupert was struck by the range of differences between this boy and Neti, who was the same age.

"Hello, Tobias," Rupert said extending his hand.

The effect on Toby of hearing his preferred name was immediate. He freed himself from Athena's grasp and went to Rupert embracing him in a bear hug. Athena laughed at the look on Rupert's face but made no apology for her brother's behaviour.

"I love you," Toby declared, burying his head into Rupert's chest.

With that embrace, Rupert felt as if something tightly knotted within him was unravelling. Not since Ross had anyone held him or told him that he was loved, and since Ross's death, Rupert had been reeling in his emotions. He now felt strangely vulnerable in the arms of this boy.

Toby finally released Rupert from his grip and returned to his sister, this time not hiding his face but smiling broadly at Rupert. A small, awkward silence followed in which Rupert became acutely aware of his unannounced presence in Athena's home. He stumbled over an apology and looked to leave, but Athena wouldn't hear of it and invited him to share the meal she had been preparing for herself and Toby. Rupert declined at first but was easily persuaded by her gentle insistence.

Despite his initial embarrassment, Rupert soon relaxed in the company of Toby and Athena. She seemed self-contained and content preparing the meal, while Rupert, at Toby's insistence, sat with him on the floor, piecing together a large and surprisingly intricate jigsaw puzzle, which Toby tackled with zeal and precision.

There was little talking between the three of them, and it was in this silence, dense with its peace, that Rupert felt the recognition of something he thought was lost to him.

Over their meal, the conversation was lightweight. Toby dominated as he related the events of his school-day to them, forgetting, at times, that Rupert did not know the people who coloured it. As he listened, Rupert was touched by the immense significance these people and events had for Toby.

Afterwards, when Athena refused Rupert's offers of help to clean up, he joined Toby on the floor, listening to him as he practised his reading. Although it was not late, Toby soon tired and Athena, who was acutely attuned to her brother's needs, readied him for bed. Although he offered token objections to this, he needed little persuasion. Once in bed, however, he gained a second wind, and called for Rupert to come in to say goodnight again. Athena, tucking her brother into his bed, raised her eyebrows to Rupert in mock frustration.

"Read me a story 'Thenie," he said, smiling charmingly.

"Not tonight," she said, bending to kiss him, "we have a visitor, remember?"

"Rupert, will you read me a story?"

Athena laughed aloud at her brother's guile and the corresponding look of surprise on Rupert's face.

Rupert accepted the book that Toby was already handing to him and sat on the edge of his bed. Athena left them and for the next fifteen minutes Rupert read to him about trains of the world, a subject, he discovered, about which Toby was very well informed.

Although Toby fought sleep, his eyelids became too heavy. Rupert closed the book and sat for a moment watching him. He thought of his own childhood, but when his thoughts turned to his father, he immediately steered them away and replaced them with those of Matthew. He felt hollow at the thought of life without his dearest friend. He left the sleeping boy and went out to Athena who had poured two cups of tea and was setting them on the dining table.

"Finally asleep I take it?" she said as she sat down. Rupert joined her. "That was very good of you to read to him."

"I enjoyed it," he said and meant it.

"Are you okay?"

Rupert coloured at her question but told her about his news regarding Matthew. He was conscious that, for someone who had lived a very uneventful and peaceful life for the past twenty years, he now seemed to constantly have a tale of woe, and it was all too easy to tell Athena about it. He wondered about the cause of misfortune, or indeed, if there was a cause at all. Some, whose lives were filled with fortune, would say that people brought bad luck upon themselves. Rupert acknowledged too, that he had sometimes thought the same when in his role as College Chaplain. Now, however, he thought more cynically that the only justice in misfortune is that it does not discriminate; it more often arrives unannounced, and is rarely, if ever, welcomed.

He voiced some of these thoughts aloud and Athena listened to him intently.

"But life is not always out of your control," she said at last, "you can change your attitude to the things that happen."

Rupert looked perplexed and was not sure if she was stating a New Age philosophy.

Athena saw his confusion and continued, "For example, when Toby was born, it could have been devastating ..." Her voice trailed off while she thought.

Rupert considered what she was saying.

"In some circumstances, it would be."

She nodded in agreement. "However, it's the attitude we take to what we see as misfortune that determines the depth of its tragedy." Athena could see she wasn't making herself clear. "Things happen in life ... not *for* a reason. *We* give the meaning to the things that happen to us. If I might borrow from Christianity and the concept of Free Will, we choose the response we make, that's our freedom."

Rupert listened to her with admiration. "You're very wise," he said, smiling. "Your parents, too, were wise in their choice of your name."

Athena laughed. "I think the choice was more to do with some hippy notion about exotic names and breaking from the mainstream, to be honest, but thanks for the compliment anyway."

Despite his heavy heart, Rupert once again felt buoyed in

Athena's presence and, though he had to leave to prepare for the journey the next day, he did so reluctantly.

Athena walked him to the door, but this time, as he was about to leave, she gripped his arm and, reaching up, kissed him softly on the cheek.

"Safe journey, Rupert."

She was still on her toes, whispering into his ear; he bent down to her and returned the kiss to her lips.

My back is *aching*. Kat closed her eyes against the dragging sensation, and the nausea that swept over her in waves. It bemused her that the symptoms could replicate so exactly, fifteen years later. What had been forgotten as soon as possible after Neti's birth, now returned as a grim reminder of what was to come. She'd sensed it though. The tightness of her breasts, the craving for red meat though she was vegetarian and a physical awkwardness that made her feel swollen and clumsy, already.

She could feel, too, her own mood swings becoming more pronounced; the medication she regularly took having little effect. Trying to contain them, especially in Rupert's presence, was draining her and caused her to speak too excitedly to compensate for the depression she was experiencing.

Neti had not seemed to notice. She was a good girl, a good daughter and she deserved a better mother, as Kat had known from the beginning.

When she saw her daughter for the first time in ten years, she could not relate to her. Neti had been Ross's child during that time. She had adopted so many of his characteristics, apparent even on that first day, and Kat could feel his presence between them.

Kat slumped back into the couch and groaned inwardly. She ran her hands across her abdomen, aware of its fullness already. She thought of herself doing the same thing, in this same room, fifteen years earlier. A wave of despair came over her and she closed her eyes against it.

———

Was he half full or half empty? Rupert wondered that as he drove the short distance home. The night was full of conflicting emotions equal in their strength.

He opened the front door and entered quietly, though he suspected that Kat would be in front of the television rather than in bed. Surprisingly, she wasn't, but he could hear her talking on the telephone in the kitchen. He hadn't planned to listen, simply to let her know that he was home, but as he approached the door, he could hear that the conversation was tense and the stilted way in which Kat was answering suggested that she was crying.

"But I *can't* come," she said, her voice cracking with sobs and sounding strangely child-like, "and you mustn't ..."

Kat's pause suggested that there was a lengthy reply. He felt both embarrassed and guilty that he was overhearing a personal conversation and steered away from the kitchen and back to the lounge room. He could still hear Kat sobbing and felt awkward and uneasy about the tone of her conversation.

He took a notepad and pen from a dresser drawer and wrote a note to Neti. Although he expected to be back before she returned home, he felt he should let her know why he needed to go away, in case he was longer than he thought. He knew she wouldn't care, but he wrote it anyway. He took it into her room. Despite Neti's often haphazard appearance and behaviour, her bedroom was surprisingly tidy. Rupert went to place it on the bed and noticed two photographs lying side by side, where Neti had apparently been looking at them before she left. Guiltily, he picked them up. One was a photograph of Ross, Kat and Neti, taken when she was just born. The other, he saw with surprise, was the recent photograph she had taken of the three of them — Neti, Kat and Rupert.

"Oh Neti," Rupert sighed, sitting heavily on the bed.

On his way back to the lounge room, Kat nearly collided with him as she headed to her room. She was obviously startled to see him and tried to hide her face, but he had already seen that her eyes were puffy and red from crying. She lowered her head and muttered a greeting but tried to get past him as quickly as possible.

"What's wrong, Kat?"

She half-turned her body towards him and seemed to be trying to determine what he knew, what he might have heard. Rupert had asked the question innocently enough, but he felt that something was terribly wrong.

She hesitated and then turned to face him. He could see her distress clearly enough now.

"Oh, I was talking to my friend in Townsville ..." She seemed to be considering what she would say next. "She had some sad news ... about another friend of ours ..."

Rupert felt that this was untrue. He wanted to tell her that but felt that he had no right. There was something unnerving about Kat that made him uneasy. He wished he didn't have to go away but knew he must. At least Neti would not be home for a few more days, he thought. He resolved to come back as quickly as possible.

That night, he tossed and turned, thinking of Matthew; seeing his friend would not be soon enough. On several occasions he heard Kat move about the house. He thought he could hear her whispering in the kitchen on one occasion and got up.

Although it was two o'clock in the morning, she was talking on the telephone and, although he could not hear what she was saying, he suspected that she was speaking to the same person.

He lay awake for some time after that, wondering what, if anything, he should do. Eventually sleep came through exhaustion.

He is standing on the cliff, where once he had held Ross in his arms. Neti is on one side of him, Matthew on the other, and they are looking out to sea. Neti and Matthew jump, leaving Rupert behind. He yells and leaps from the cliff after them. They are falling and Rupert is reaching out trying to catch Neti with one hand and Matthew with the other. As they fall further away, they turn to look at him. Both are wearing Ross's face ... or is it his? They are too far from him now, moving out of sight. Rupert lands on soft ground but he cannot see Neti or Matthew. Athena is there. She is stroking his forehead.

"Neti is alright," she says, and he trusts her.

"And Matthew?" he pleads.

She shakes her head. She does not know.

CHAPTER SEVEN

Long, winding roads gave birth to long, winding thoughts. The drive to the Community lulled Rupert into reminiscences of Matthew. Occasionally, Rupert checked himself, not wanting to tempt fate, but a part of him feared that Matthew would die soon, and Rupert's mind was already moving into its own particular therapy and its need to begin at the beginning.

The hotel's doors were wide open to let in the summer breeze or, it seemed to Rupert, to let out the stale, yeasty smell of old and newly spilt beer, cigarettes and the bodies that consumed both. The voices that swam out to the street on the tide of odours were particularly merry on this Friday afternoon. Final examinations had been completed, the university year was over, and the first-year students now were unleashing their more reckless selves in time for Christmas festivities.

This wasn't necessarily true for Ross. Rupert would be able to find him here on any Friday evening during the year, and that night, he would be as reckless as on any other of those nights. He marvelled at his brother's endless revelry and his ability to match Rupert's first-class grades in studies that, in Rupert's case, were achieved through swatting and abstinence.

Rupert was jostled as he manoeuvred through the large crowd to Ross's usual roost by the bar where he would hold court. He wasn't there.

"Hello there, Ross."

Rupert spun around to the mention of his brother's name. A middle-aged man, whose face looked permanently etched with expressions of pleasure, was extending his hand.

"You're not Ross," the man said still smiling and grasped Rupert's hand, "but you must be Rupert?"

Rupert responded immediately to the physical and emotional warmth of the gesture and knew, in the fleeting moment of contact, that he liked this man.

"It's somewhat unnerving, the face times two," he said laughing and released Rupert's hand, "but you must be tired of people confusing the two of you."

"Well, we have no trouble in telling ourselves apart," Rupert answered with a wry smile. He noticed a discreet crucifix pinned to the collar of the man's white sport shirt.

"I'm Matthew," the man said more loudly over the sudden increase in the din of the revellers. He saw Rupert look at his lapel, "Father Matthew Gallagher. I'm a friend of Ross."

Rupert's eyebrows shot upwards.

Matthew laughed, his face becoming a concertina of wrinkles.

"And that's taken you by surprise."

Rupert was bewildered and Matthew offered him a drink as compensation.

They sat outside at a wooden table in the late afternoon breeze and Rupert heard the story of the unlikely friendship between his capricious brother and this priest. He learned that

Ross and Matthew had become acquainted three months previously. Matthew came from a local church, and on Friday nights he often visited this hotel that serviced locals, workers and university students. It was his way of making connections in a less formal setting and, he admitted with a wink, not a bad way to spend a Friday evening.

It had not taken long for Ross to settle into the swing of the University social scene and to find his way to its favoured watering-hole where he and Matthew met.

Ross held court amongst the other students. He was witty and lively, but then would sit quietly on his own in the corner. Matthew approached him there one evening. Though Ross was initially reluctant to talk, before too long they were conversing.

What Matthew learned of Ross in that and subsequent conversations, he did not say, but Rupert felt a pang of envy, if not betrayal, at the thought that his twin might share intimate thoughts with another, thoughts that Rupert may not have been aware his brother held. From the understanding looks that Matthew gave him, Rupert wondered what Ross had told Matthew about himself.

Yet Rupert could understand that his brother might open up to this man. Though there was a gentility about him, it seemed to Rupert that Matthew had had his own experiences that perhaps enabled him to understand the failings of others.

The morning sun muted the greens of the valley. He loved this drive, the route so often taken in the days when he was full of enthusiasm and he would make the reverse trip, from the Community to Matthew in Melbourne.

In that first meeting at the hotel, Rupert and Matthew began a friendship that grew, over time, to a deep love and respect. Rupert had responded immediately to Matthew's warmth and understanding. Partly this was born out of Rupert's need, and therefore his readiness, to listen to the counsel of an older man. But it was more than his words. Amid Matthew's humour and his apparent worldliness, Rupert recognized a deep commitment to Christian values, not in the evangelical tone of his own father, but in everything about him. He was a living example of the values that Rupert had been precariously on the edge of rejecting in retaliation against his father.

In subsequent meetings, the older man reintroduced the younger to the Church in its Catholic face, and Rupert took readily to its elaborate rituals and its paradoxical simplicity. Ross was pleased that Rupert and Matthew had struck up a friendship, recognizing his brother's needs, but he blamed Matthew for the choice that Rupert would eventually make that took him away for twelve years.

As he drove, Rupert inhaled the freshness of the hay and eucalyptus, drawing a long, unlaboured breath for the second time in the last two days. He thought of the night before — of Athena — and blushed at the fact that he had kissed her. A rush of pleasure at the thought of her surprised him.

He breathed deeply of the day, each exhalation causing him to relax, and yet he was on his way to visit his dying friend. But the sight and smell of the fields, so full of optimism on this cloudless morning, and the presence of Matthew waiting for him at the end of the journey, though it might be the last, brought him some peace.

The gates stood open in an arms-stretched welcome. *The Prodigal Son.*

Had these gates ever been closed? The rusty stakes and the smugly settled plants that hugged them told him otherwise. He thought about the first time he had come in through these gates. How eager he was, how arrogant in his certainty. He remembered how he had wished these same gates would close tightly behind him, locking out the world and, most especially, his father. Rupert had looked back over his shoulder on that day, fearful that he would be there to stop him at the last moment, breaking his vow never to speak to Rupert again. He didn't come, nor did he ever speak, not even the last time as they stood over the grave of the woman who had linked them in blood.

Rupert thought of Kat's recent, unwanted advice about his father. He had not told her that he'd tried to tell him about Ross's death, but had been informed, sympathetically by a staff member, that his father did not want to see him.

Parking the car, Rupert felt anxious. *The Prodigal Son* ... the thought kept recurring. Ridiculous! He admonished himself. They didn't know here that he was not the same unquestioning youth who had left years before.

"I am not coming back in humility," he said aloud. He shut the car door harder than he intended.

There was an unreality about the walk from the car to the main building that served as an ad hoc reception area for visitors who attended the retreat programs offered here. Today, Rupert felt as though he was seeing this entire place for the first time, brought on by the knowledge that it might be the last. There was little that offered a comforting sense of the known, of belonging; Rupert could feel Matthew's presence strongly already. The complacency that overtook him on the drive there was suddenly overtaken by an increased urgency to see his friend. His step quickened.

Dominic, a young seminarian Rupert had met on previous visits, crossed the path ahead and, seeing Rupert, veered towards him.

"I'm so glad to see you," he said clasping Rupert's hand in his.

Rupert scrutinised Dominic's face. "How's Matthew?" He was almost afraid to ask.

Dominic shook his head. "It won't be long, Rupert. We've made him as comfortable as we can."

"Shouldn't he be in the hospital?" Rupert could hear his voice rising but did not want to offend Dominic.

"Matthew wants to be here," Dominic said gently and with understanding, "there's little that can be done for him now."

The two men walked in the direction of the building where Matthew lay dying.

"He's conscious and asking for you, Rupert. That is, he's asking for Elijah."

"You knew that was me?" Rupert said with a heavy heart.

"Oh yes. Matthew spoke of you often, and his name for you."

Inside the residential building, Dominic directed Rupert to a glassed room that opened onto a sun-filled courtyard. As they approached, Rupert could see the loved figure of Matthew hunched in his wheelchair in the sun, a blanket wrapped around his thin and frail body. They paused at the window and Rupert leaned his forehead on the glass and soaked in the sight of his friend and mentor.

"He's asleep," Dominic whispered and, seeing the look on Rupert's face, patted him on the back and walked away.

Rupert sat on the ground beside Matthew who had still not stirred, his head bowed forward over his chest. He looked up into the old man's face, absorbing every detail of him, entrusting it to his memory. Matthew was pale, the bottom lip that jutted out slightly in his sleep was tinged with blue and was wet from the dribble of a deep sleep. His breathing was sharp and made small whistling sounds as he exhaled. The wrinkles of his face were permanently etched as evidence of a life filled with laughter. Rupert knew that Matthew's life had not always been as peaceful as his latter days proved to be, but he met all his obstacles with grace and, when possible, with humour. He had entrusted his life to the God he loved and, as a result, saw misfortune in the context of a full life, a life he was honoured to have been given.

Matthew's hands rested on his lap, one lying over the other. Rupert took one in his own and stroked along the prominent veins at its back. He had never noticed before how long Matthew's fingers were and wondered that it would be possible to not know something like that about someone you love. He raised the hand and placed the palm against his own face. Though the skin was cool, he could feel Matthew's life still warm at its centre. Keeping the palm pressed to his cheek, Rupert rested his head on Matthew's knee.

Matthew's free hand twitched and stirred, and Rupert felt it lay across his hair.

"Elijah?" Matthew's feeble voice whispered to him.

Rupert hesitated, wanting to prolong the moments now.

"It's me, Matthew," he said eventually, turning to look up into the old man's face. Matthew's soft brown eyes were dulled, but it seemed to Rupert that something clear lay behind them.

He placed the older man's hands into his frail lap and came up onto his knees to better see his friend.

"Are you warm enough?" he said, making unnecessary adjustments to the blanket.

Matthew smiled weakly and coughed more weakly still.

"You look tired ..." he said to Rupert and they both smiled at the irony, "you miss your brother."

Rupert leaned into the blanket tucked at Matthew's shoulder.

Matthew rested his head against the younger man. "Where are you?" he said softly.

"I'm here, Matthew."

Matthew raised a frail arm and lightly touched Rupert on the chest. "Where is your heart, Elijah?"

The touch threatened to produce tears, but Rupert checked himself for fear that every word or gesture from Matthew would find a hole in the dyke. He looked away. He could not answer.

Matthew's hand brought an unsteady finger to his lips. "Listen ... Look."

Rupert sat attentively, wondering what it was that Matthew wanted him to hear and see. A small breeze rustled through the courtyard.

After several minutes, he looked at Matthew, expecting to find him asleep. Though his lids were heavy, he was looking ahead.

"What did the wind bring you, Elijah?"

Rupert was silent and bemused.

Huskily, Matthew repeated his question.

Rupert didn't know what to say, but Matthew had fallen asleep, his breath wheezing in his throat.

Rupert sat down on the grass and leaned against the arm of the wheelchair. He didn't understand what Matthew was asking and thought that perhaps it was a sign of his senility.

The late morning sun was like a balm on his face and body. The breeze blew across the yard in short, gentle bursts. Through hooded lids he perused his surroundings. Tidy garden beds lovingly tended were still holding onto the summer's now ageing blooms. He was glad they had not yet been culled.

The breeze stopped. Unseen birds chirped in the distance. On a new puff of wind, a crimson and yellow leaf floated to his feet. He picked it up, looking for the tree to which it belonged, but the few trees in the courtyard had not yet dressed for autumn. He studied it and turned it over, running his fingers along the veins on its pale back. They yielded to his gentle pressure, as Matthew's had. He held the leaf in the flattened palm of his hand, and it drifted away from him on a new draught. He wondered what else the wind would bring him but could already feel the demand in his expectation. He let it go and waited. The wind brought nothing. He waited. He felt nothing. He waited. And for the briefest of moments, he was nothing ... but the wind and the chirp of unseen birds.

Matthew twitched and muttered in his sleep. Rupert tended him, securing again the blanket around him. Matthew opened his eyes and drew a painful intake of air. Close to Rupert's ear he whispered slowly:

Upon my flowering breast
Which I kept wholly for Him alone
There he lay sleeping

He paused, longer this time, and continued with effort:

And I caressing Him
There in a breeze from the fanning cedars.

So long it was since Rupert had heard these lines or thought of them, but he responded immediately:

When the breeze blew from the turret
Parting His hair,
He wounded my neck
With His gentle hand,
Suspending all my senses.

Matthew smiled and nodded and fell back into sleep, exhausted.

Rupert pondered the next and last stanza but could not remember it. The work had been immensely important to him in the stages of his conversion to Catholicism under Matthew's guidance; so important that he had travelled to Spain to visit the sites famous in the life of its sixteenth-century author, the mystic St. John of the Cross. His life and his works had inspired Rupert, not the least reason being that the saint's poetry was partly the result of his own darkness — he knew the struggle to believe, the dark night of the soul. How ironic, Rupert thought, that now that he was living his own darkness, he could not remember the lines. He suspected that in his own case, the inner light had been extinguished.

The day with Matthew was spent peacefully in the garden and then inside when the wind became cooler. Matthew slept for much of it, occasionally opening his eyes to find the face of the younger man who sat dutifully by him, and then drifting back to sleep contentedly. For Rupert the day was not slow enough. He absorbed the presence of his friend as if storing him for the long drought ahead. He feared the drought, feared the dearth of his emotional resources, and wondered if it was himself who was going to die. It wasn't that he wanted to die, it was just that he couldn't envisage his future and felt that perhaps he was having a premonition of his own early death.

Frequently, Dominic came by to check that Matthew and Rupert were comfortable. Rupert fed Matthew a thin vegetable soup that, surprisingly, he sipped with interest.

"I'd rather a beer," he said, with a lazy half-wink between spoonfuls.

"Not a whisky?" Rupert responded with mock and genuine surprise.

"We can all change, Elijah," Matthew answered with the smallest, mischievous smile.

Rupert pondered the name that Matthew had fondly given him many years before. The two men had met frequently following their initial meeting at the hotel. In the course of one evening, Rupert told Matthew about the experience that he had had on the bluff the year before. He had not told anyone else, except Ross who had not remembered much about the evening and thought that Rupert must also have had too much to drink. Despite Rupert's protestations Ross dismissed it and was uncharacteristically curt with his brother when Rupert told him about 'the voice'. Matthew had listened to Rupert's description of the visual experience but more intently to his recounting of the voice that he knew that he had heard. When Rupert had finished, Matthew recounted the passage of 1 Kings where Elijah, standing on the mountain, heard the still small voice of God.

Just as he had done when recounting the story of his experience to Athena, Rupert now inwardly cringed at the memory of it. He didn't know what to make of it anymore. He thought of Athena's research and her conviction that our brain's chemistry is responsible for such perceived phenomena. If this was so ... He blushed at the thought of it. And yet, as he spooned in another mouthful of soup, he pondered Matthew's gentle and trusting face and wondered.

Dominic had prepared a room for Rupert, but he preferred to sleep with Matthew in his small room. When Matthew had been lifted out of the wheelchair and placed in his bed, Rupert sponged the old man's pale and age-blemished body. Though weak, Matthew giggled like a child being tickled, as Rupert sponged under one arm.

Once Matthew was comfortable and asleep, Rupert left him to telephone Kat.

"Hello," came the feeble response to his ringing.

"Kat?"

Rupert was concerned at the tone of her voice. It was still early evening, only six o'clock, and yet Kat sounded as though he had woken her from a heavy sleep. Either that or she was unwell.

"It's Rupert, Kat. Are you alright?"

"Yes ... " she said groggily, and then "yes," more forcefully.

"Have you heard from Neti?"

"Who?"

"Neti, Kat. Have you heard from her?" Rupert couldn't hide the exasperation in his voice.

"No ... No ... She's not due home yet, is she?" Kat sounded confused.

"No." Rupert was certain this was met with "Thank God" at the other end.

"Are you sure you're alright?"

"*Yes Rupert!* For God's sake! I'm okay! What do you want, anyway?"

Rupert hesitated, unsure what to say. "Nothing really. I just wanted to make sure that ... "

"What? That I haven't screwed everything up?" Kat's voice, which had lost its grogginess, now sounded bitter.

"No ... No." Rupert was shocked that she said it, but he had to admit to himself that there was some truth in her statement.

"When are you home?" she said matter-of-factly.

"I'll stay again tomorrow night if that's all right with you?"

"Suit yourself."

He could not fail to notice the sharp tone in her voice. He couldn't understand why she was talking this way. At least Neti would not be home for another two days, he thought as he put down the telephone.

That night, Rupert barely slept. Instead, he dozed in the armchair beside Matthew in between checks on his welfare, a task normally done by the Community brothers in a rotating system. He was dozing when he was startled awake by the sound of Matthew's voice, clear and loud.

"Elijah!"

Rupert leapt from the chair, fearing the worst, but instead found Matthew wide awake and alert.

"Turn up the brightness," he said wheezing, indicating the lamp that was glowing dully on the small table in the corner.

Rupert switched on the overhead light.

"In the drawer ..." Matthew nodded in the direction of the table.

Rupert obeyed, wondering if there was some medication Matthew needed urgently. The only thing in the drawer was Matthew's now old and lovingly worn Bible, which Rupert recognized immediately. He took it out and ran his hand over the brown leather cover, his thoughts becoming a mixture of memories of the times when Matthew had read to him from it. He felt loose inside.

"Solomon ... the Song," Matthew ordered with husky breath.

Rupert wondered what Matthew wanted here. It was not a Book that the two of them had shared. The pages opened easily with a photograph of a woman inserted at Chapters 4 to 6.

"Four, nine to eleven," Matthew said, reaching a shaking hand for the photograph.

Rupert read dutifully,

"You have ravished my heart, my sister, my bride,
you have ravished my heart with a glance of your eyes,
with one jewel of your necklace.
How sweet is your love, my sister, my bride!
how much better is your love than wine,
and the fragrance of your oils than any spice!
Your lips distil nectar, my bride;

honey and milk are under your tongue;
the scent of your garments is like the scent of Lebanon."

As he read, Rupert glanced at Matthew who silently mouthed the words as he read them.When he had finished, he waited self-consciously, not understanding why Matthew had asked him to read this passage but suspecting that it had something to do with the woman in the photograph.

"We were to marry," Matthew said, as if reading his thoughts, holding the photograph out to him.

Despite his suspicions, Rupert twitched with surprise and shock. He studied the woman in the now aged-yellowed photograph. Though not a beauty, her face, in her thirties at least, was striking for the clarity of her eyes and the mischievous smile, which Rupert thought was probably directed to Matthew as the photographer, a Matthew that he didn't know had existed.

Although the two men were very close, it became apparent to Rupert that perhaps he knew little about his friend's life. Matthew was a wonderful listener, and in that capacity, he had created an atmosphere in which Rupert felt secure in telling him his most intimate thoughts. He realised now that perhaps this had not been reciprocated. Though he knew many factual details of Matthew's life, there were obviously things he had not shared — until now.

Matthew watched his younger friend as he stared at the photograph.

"Do we ever really know the deepest dreams of another, Elijah?"

"You know mine," Rupert answered him still not looking up, his voice husky. He placed the photograph in Matthew's hand and stroked the silver hair from his damp brow. "Tell me about her."

Painfully and with a great deal of effort, Matthew related the story of the one woman he had loved — Clare. He told Rupert how they had met and fallen in love, had become engaged, but how he had also felt drawn to religious life, the choice he was ultimately to make over her. He knew he could not give her one hundred per cent of himself and that she deserved more than this. Although he loved her, and continued to love her, he had felt that God would better understand the tug of two loves on his heart.

"Perhaps I was wrong, Elijah. She may well have understood. I know now... that the human heart ... has a great capacity for understanding ... and love."

"Do you regret your decision, Matthew?"

Matthew hesitated and Rupert could feel himself tensing in anticipation of an answer he was not sure he wanted to hear.

"I struggled," Matthew's breathing was laboured, but he was alert and lucid. "I struggled." His eyes became glazed.

Rupert lowered his, aware that Matthew was for that moment in the memory of his love.

"You miss her still."

Matthew smiled. "Yes ... but I found peace ... with my God .... It's the little things ... in a marriage ... that make all the difference ... The little comforts ... like well-loved slippers .... We have that ...God ... and ... me." He brought the photograph to his chest.

Rupert was about to ask what happened to Clare. Did she marry? Was she still alive? but Matthew had fallen asleep exhausted from his effort. His fingers lay curled around the photograph.

Though weary from lack of sleep, Rupert sat by the bed for the next hour, his thoughts drifting loosely. As he leaned forward in his chair and rested his head and arms on the bed, the final stanza that had eluded him earlier spoke loudly in his head:

> *I abandoned and forgot myself,*
> *Laying my face on my Beloved;*
> *All things ceased; I went out from myself,*
> *Leaving my cares*
> *Forgotten among the lilies.*

CHAPTER EIGHT

N eti hung up the telephone.

"Everything all right, love?"

"Yep," she said, "Kat's home."

Despite Neti's reassurance, Polly's mother wasn't convinced and gave a look to her husband. He answered with a silence.

"Is your uncle home?"

Neti rolled her eyes, "Probably."

"Are you sure you don't want to stay another night?"

"Go on, Net," Polly said from behind her parents, still eating her lunch at the table.

Neti smiled at her friend's enthusiasm, but she wanted to go home to spend some time with her mother. She was worried though. Kat had sounded vague and distressed on the telephone and Neti had to repeat herself several times in the short conversation. She must have another migraine, she thought to herself.

"I think I'll go home, thanks. Rupert mightn't be there after all."

Penny's mother shot another look at her husband, who raised his eyebrows in resignation. He picked up his car keys.

"C'mon then, love. I'll take you home."

On the way, Neti felt the stirrings of something she couldn't name, but it made her feel uneasy. Once at her front door though, she turned and waved to Polly and her father with a reassuring smile, despite her own uncertainty.

The house was silent when she entered. The lounge room was dark and stuffy and had an unfamiliar, unpleasant odour. A pillow and blanket were askew on the couch as if someone had just got up from sleeping there. Neti looked around. Kat's now trademark coffee cup was on the floor and had been knocked; sediment had spilt on the carpet. Another cup sat on the table, half full of milky coffee that had formed a day-old scum.

She looked for her mother in the kitchen; there was little disturbed there, except for an unwiped bench and a plate with a half-eaten sandwich on the sink.

Neti heard someone retching in the toilet and knocked on the door.

"*What?*" Kat's voice was garbled.

Neti opened the door tentatively. "Kat? Are you okay?"

Her mother was on her knees over the toilet and retching into the bowl. Exhausted, she sat back on her haunches and rested her forehead on her arms.

Vomit-stiffened hair was stuck to Kat's mouth and face. She smelt horribly and was still wearing the dress in which she had waved Neti goodbye, three days earlier. She groaned. Neti sat beside her but reeled back from the smell. She waited to see if Kat was able to stand. The two sat together in silence, Kat still not acknowledging that her daughter was there.

After a few minutes, when the nausea had eased, Neti helped Kat from the floor. She led her towards Kat's bedroom, but she refused to go and, shrugging Neti off, headed for her make-shift bed on the couch.

"Should I call a doctor?" Neti said, smoothing the blanket over her mother, all the time wondering where Rupert could be.

"No!"

When Kat was finally asleep, Neti cleaned up the lounge room. She wasn't certain what to do but hoped that Rupert could not be far. She went into her bedroom and opened a window and, before she could see the note he had written her, a breeze blew it out of her sight.

Neti sat on the bed to wait for her uncle to return home.

Athena riffled through the papers on her desk. Several subjects had been interviewed, and there were many other documented cases to draw on. Each person's heightened religious experience had been so different — the age at which it had occurred, the location of the experience, the life circumstances, the mental state at the time. But one factor was common: the certainty that the experience happened as told and the overriding, overwhelming emotion that accompanied it. The sense of awe remained with each, except for Rupert, it seemed.

Athena studied the data from Rupert's interview. His mother's alcoholism held particular interest for her, and even more so because Rupert's identical twin also suffered this condition. Interestingly, it had manifested at the same time that Rupert had had his experience, but Athena didn't know what to make of the loose connection. This area of neuroscience was proving to be as difficult as she had envisaged. She often wondered why she had chosen it — results of work already done were inconclusive, as much of the scientific research involving human consciousness tended to be. But she was fascinated by the recording of such experiences throughout the history of modern man. Athena felt certain that the cause was physical and wanted to prove it. The limitation, and the frustration, was that there was still so much more to know about the brain. At best, there was a possible location responsible for religious experience. Similar events to those experienced by Athena's subjects, and those from previous studies, could be simulated in the laboratory by stimulating the temporal lobe. What might serve as the stimulus outside the laboratory though was still under question and was the basis of her research.

She picked up a letter and read again the bursary offer from the University of Pennsylvania. It would assist her research immeasurably, but there were several factors to consider if she was to accept it, not the least leaving her brother. She knew she must make the decision now.

Her thoughts homed in on her last meeting with Rupert and his kiss. It had been so unexpected, and he'd left so quickly that she wondered, briefly, if it had happened at all. The memory of it brought her pleasure and she allowed herself to revel in it. But when she thought about it more rationally, taking into account his emotional state and, more particularly, his vocation, she berated herself for her own foolishness. Athena looked again at the letter in front of her, picked up her pen and, hesitating briefly, completed the last section of the form.

———

An hour had passed and there had been no word from Rupert.

Mercifully, Kat slept. When Neti checked on her, she found her mother in an almost unnaturally deep sleep; her mouth hung open and her breathing was erratic.

Neti busied herself washing the clothes she had taken away and the towels that had lay damp, smelling of early mildew, on the bathroom floor.

Another hour passed. Kat didn't respond to offers of food and so Neti settled to making herself a sandwich from three-day-old bread.

The house was unsettlingly quiet. When it had been just herself and her father living here, there had been noise. He had been a lively and talkative man; so different from his brother. Neti thought of the times she would come home from school and Ross would be there, early from work, waiting for her. The house would be clean and bright and he suspiciously brighter. He seemed to always be sucking a mint, but it failed to disguise the smell of alcohol when she kissed him hello.

Neti tipped the remnants of her sandwich into the bin that was peppered with ants. She went into her uncle's bedroom; she hoped that she could find a clue as to where he could be. She tried to remember the name of his 'girlfriend' as her mother had referred to her. The name, Neti remembered, was unusual and had made her think of a television program about a warrior princess. She ran through the alphabet to prompt her memory as she began to search his room.

If it's here, it won't be too hard to find, Neti thought, as she began at the polished dresser. In the need for cleanliness, her uncle most resembled her father. For other people, she knew, it was their physical resemblance. But Neti never had trouble distinguishing the two when they were together. Alcohol and grief had etched different lines on her father's face, but so had his laughter.

She wondered about the quiet and unhappy man who now inhabited this room. When she looked around at its simplicity, its order, she felt a compulsion to throw it in disarray. Neti hesitated, aware that thoughts such as these were erupting frequently. Gingerly, she moved the few items on the dresser, but found nothing. She opened the wardrobe door, but again there was little to be found, except a small cardboard box, an assemble-yourself type, that was on the floor beside a single pair of shoes. Neti took it out and placed it on the bed. It was half-filled with letters, cards and other paperwork. She emptied the contents and, on one envelope, recognized the handwriting. It was in her father's hand, written to Rupert at an address she didn't know. The postmark was ten years old. With a trembling hand she extracted the letter but knew she couldn't cope with hearing it read in her father's voice and pushed it abruptly back into its envelope and into the box.

Neti moved the other items on the bed aside, looking for the information she wanted — a name and telephone number. She saw her own name written on an envelope. The card inside was covered in coloured balloons that carried the message, *'Happy 15th Birthday'*. She was puzzled. Her fifteenth birthday had been a few days before Kat had arrived. She remembered that she had chosen not to spend the evening with her uncle, telling him that she would go to Polly's instead. He'd been cooking and, she remembered, there was a birthday cake with candles in the refrigerator that he had made her. Neti winced at the memory and tried to recall if he had given her a card. He had. It was plainer than the one in her hand and expressed simply inside, *"To dear Neti ... love from Rupert"*, the sentiments of an unknown writer filling the space between.

She opened this card and read it.

"To dearest Neti,

How I wish for you a year of happiness,
How I wish for you a year of peace.
I pray that we find it together.

With all my love,
Rupert."

In the reading of it, Neti sensed her uncle's awkwardness. Thoughtfully, she put it back into its envelope and placed it carefully in the box.

Rifling through the remaining papers, she finally found what was needed.

"Athena!" she said.

Replacing the other items into the box, Neti returned it to its exact position in the wardrobe.

The final beep of the answering machine greeted Athena and Toby as they came through the front door.

"I'll check the messages, Tobe ... You run a bath, okay?"

Toby saluted her and dutifully headed for the bathroom.

Athena smiled to herself. Toby and his friends from school were perfecting their salutes in Forrest Gump style; they'd seen some of the movie as a special treat. Fortunately, Athena thought, this fascination with military life was also leading to absolute obedience. She hoped this fad would last a while.

The telephone messages played while Athena prepared dinner. The last one stopped her, the knife in her hand suspended above the chopping board.

"Hello ... Um ... It's Neti Brown ... I'm looking for Rupert Brown ... My uncle."

Athena was puzzled. Why would Rupert's niece call her? Why would she think he was here? She played the message again. The young girl's voice was unsteady, and Athena sensed that there was something wrong. She pressed buttons on the telephone to recall the last telephone number.

A small, anxious voice answered.

"Neti, it's Athena Nevis ... Is everything all right?"

The relief in the girl's voice was palpable. She told Athena that her mother was ill, that she didn't know what to do and that she didn't know where her uncle could be.

"He's visiting a sick friend in the country, Neti." Athena wondered that Rupert had not told her. She pressed for more details about Neti's mother's condition and became concerned. "I think I should come," she said matter-of-factly, and Neti did not hesitate to give the address.

Toby, scrubbed and rosy, couldn't believe his luck that his health-conscious sister was permitting take-away. He sat with a military back in the car's passenger seat, carefully guarding the plastic cartons balanced between his legs.

"Who's Neti, again?"

"Rupert's niece."

Toby smiled broadly at the mention of the older man's name.

"But don't forget, Rupert won't be there," Athena reminded him.

She was touched by Toby's immediate response to Rupert. Toby was, by nature, very affectionate and in the past had approached people with enthusiastic greetings. Several experiences of insensitive rejection had curbed that enthusiasm and sometimes made him more guarded with people. Although Rupert too had been taken aback — Athena smiled at the memory of their meeting — his eventual response had matched Toby's. Rupert had treated him with respect, as an individual, not the object of patronizing pity. The boy had talked of Rupert often since then.

"How old's Neti?"

"Your age," Athena said, raising her eyebrows at the thought of the probable discrepancy in the respective abilities of these two fifteen-year-olds. She wondered what Neti was like and how she would receive both herself and her brother.

"Behave yourself, won't you, Tobe?" she said.

The door opened immediately to Athena's knock.

Neti's hair was defiant; her smile was not, when Athena introduced herself and her brother.

"Hi ... Come in," Neti said awkwardly to both and stepped aside.

"Hi!" Toby mimicked in return, wrestling with the take-away bags.

As Athena stepped through the doorway, she felt apprehensive. What would Rupert think of her being here in his absence?

The atmosphere inside the house was oppressive. Athena could not see Neti's mother, but she could sense her presence, and, although part of her was reluctant, she followed Neti to her. Toby, staying close, looked hopefully for a sign of Rupert.

Athena knelt by the couch. Kat was conscious but seemed to drift in and out of sleep. The smell of the woman made Athena gasp for air. She felt her forehead — it was clammy and cold.

Kat opened her eyes and was startled to see an unfamiliar face. She looked beyond Athena to where Toby and Neti stood passively behind her.

Athena stroked her damp hair in reassurance. "I'm ... a friend of Rupert's. Can I help you? Do you know what's wrong?"

Kat shifted her body from the woman. "Go away."

Unfazed by the woman's abruptness, Athena directed the conversation to Neti and told her that she would call a doctor. The response from Kat was immediate and she attempted to sit up.

"No! I'm all right! I know what's wrong." She looked warily from Athena to Neti and back again.

Athena asked Neti if she would help Toby to serve the meal he was still guarding. Taking charge of the parcels, Neti invited him to help her in the kitchen. He marched behind her obediently.

Once out of view, Kat spoke lucidly.

"I'm pregnant."

Athena was not sure how to react to this news. She didn't know this woman well enough to be either shocked or delighted. But there was something in the surreptitious way in which she spoke that made Athena believe that the news could not be good. Before she could respond, Kat continued.

"I've tried to get rid of it."

There was a lunging of her insides that Athena hoped she could contain. She did not speak.

"It didn't work," Kat continued. "I know ..." She turned towards the kitchen to be sure that she could not be heard there. "I've tried it before."

Athena's mind was swimming with thoughts; most pressing though, was her concern for this woman's welfare. She urged, insisted, that Kat should see a doctor, but she would not have it.

"All right," Athena finally relented. "But I won't leave until I know you're not in any danger."

In the kitchen, Neti absorbed herself dishing up dinner, relieved that the situation with her mother now seemed to be under some control. She liked Athena immediately, but couldn't understand what she might see in her stuffy uncle. It never crossed her mind to question that Athena was Rupert's girlfriend. Though Neti only vaguely knew her grandfather, from occasional visits to the nursing home with Ross, she knew that, as a religious minister, he had married. She didn't know about her uncle's vow of chastity and assumed that he had just not found someone to love him.

At first, Neti was irritated by Toby. She strained her ears to hear the conversation taking place in the lounge room, but he constantly chattered. Once or twice, she answered sharply. Exasperated, she abruptly placed glasses on the table and set him to pouring a drink for each of them. When she turned from the cupboard with plates in her hand, she witnessed the back of him, knees bent so that his eyes were level with the rim of the glasses, carefully pouring the lemonade so that each glass would have exactly the same amount. He didn't know she was watching, and when he spilt some on the bench, she heard his soft gasp. She felt ashamed of her behaviour towards him then.

"It's okay," she said, as Toby tried to wipe away the spill with his fingers.

He beamed.

"I'll have the same as you," he told her matter-of-factly as she served the portions from the plastic containers.

"No worries." Neti smiled to herself.

Perhaps it was the comfort of Athena's presence, but Kat seemed to gain more strength and was able to sit up. Athena didn't ask questions of her, other than how she was feeling and if she was bleeding, but she could feel Kat watching her, taking her in as if putting together pieces of a mental puzzle.

"How long have you known Rupert?" Kat asked in what seemed to be an outward expression of her thoughts. The question, in itself, was innocent enough, but Athena felt that she was being steered into unknown waters, and so, after answering Kat's question, she deftly moved the conversation back to her welfare. Kat's smile suggested that she recognized the manoeuvre, and she played along.

From the kitchen, Toby's voice piped away over Neti's deeper monosyllabic answers. Kat, who had not really been in a condition to be aware of Toby's presence, raised an eyebrow quizzically.

"My brother ... Tobias," Athena explained and told her about his condition, feeling all the while a discomfort under the circumstances of Kat's confession.

It appeared that Kat felt it too, as she lowered her eyes and her face fixed into a small, defensive set, though it lacked confidence.

"You must think little of me."

Athena was taken aback by the statement and hesitated before replying.

"It's not my place to judge your decisions. I'm not in your position and can really only guess what my own choice would be, if I was."

"It's not as natural as I thought it would be," Kat said quietly, "motherhood, I mean. I truly wish it was, and I waited for the feeling to come ... but it didn't, and I don't feel the urgings, like marrow in the bones, that other women seem to feel. Is there something wrong with me?"

Athena grappled for an answer. Was there something wrong? The woman in her that would want her own child said, yes. The scientist, too, thought that it was possible. But would administering the right chemicals or gene therapy be the answer ... to *make* someone feel maternal. Athena knew that it was trite to think so, and it also demeaned the dignity of Kat's experience and genuine question.

"You know your own feelings. What can I say?"

Athena knew her response was inadequate but wanted to avoid the potential intimacy of this conversation.

From the kitchen came Neti's laugh. Kat glanced in the direction of it and lowered her voice.

"She needs a mother ... but I don't think I ..."

Before she could finish, the kitchen door opened. Neti carried a tray of plates, and Toby walked rigidly behind her, his eyes fixed on the glass he gripped in each hand.

Neti was surprised and pleased to see her mother sitting up and served her first, but Kat, still unable to eat, pushed the plate away.

"Thanks, Neti. You've done a good job," Athena said as she accepted her plate.

Toby appeared to be most pleased with the evening's arrangement and beamed with pleasure, as if he was in the company of his dearest friends.There were awkward silences amongst the others, punctuated now and then with pleasantries and the sound of Toby's exuberant chewing.

Though never comfortable with small-talk, Athena was grateful for it tonight. She wondered what she should do. Kat was stubborn in her refusal to see a doctor, but Athena couldn't leave them, especially Neti, who seemed to be more relaxed now. She watched the young girl with her mother and felt sad for what Kat had told her, and anxious for what she feared she had been about to say.

It was clear to Athena in this brief meeting that, although Kat might have good intentions, motherhood was proving to be too much for her. Neti, she observed, was a young girl trying to be older than her years. There was an element of defiance in her nature, of self-protection, and a hint of unruliness that would need to be watched, but she was kind-hearted too. Athena could see that Neti loved her mother and tried hard to please her. She saw too that Neti flinched in the face of Kat's occasional sharp-edged responses. But what struck Athena mostly, was the way in which Neti responded to Toby. As the evening progressed, she witnessed Neti becoming softer to him, even maternal to a degree, and Athena thought further about the innateness of such feelings.

She wondered how Rupert managed in this house. His niece could be a handful, and Kat probably more so, but she had the impression from him that he would rather be here than not. She suspected that there was little to offer him outside this home.

Taking in the room, its character and style, Athena realised that probably little of it represented the man who now lived here. There were photographs on the mantle shelf that she would have liked to look at closely. Athena imagined Rupert sitting in this room and decided that his armchair might be the one by the fire facing away from the television.

She felt a longing to see him.

Toby, in typical fashion, settled in quickly. Despite his almost overwhelming enthusiasm for Neti's company, he determined her measure and diluted his behaviour to suit her, so that the two of them now comfortably played Snakes and Ladders on the floor. If Neti had imagined herself to be too old for such a game, she never let on and seemed to be enjoying herself. Kat, too, seemed comfortable and wasn't at all apologetic about any possible inconvenience or awkwardness that Athena might feel.

It was a natural progression then for Athena and Toby to stay the night. When it was apparent that they would sleep in Rupert's room, Athena felt some hesitation, though she did smile to herself at the thought that he could come home and find such unlikely guests in his bed.

Kat did not intend to move from the couch. Athena straightened the cushions and found clean pillowslips to make her more comfortable. Though Kat was no longer nauseous, nor seemed to be in pain, she was very tired and settled into a deep sleep.

Toby was most pleased to be tucked into Rupert's bed.

When her brother was settled, Athena sought Neti to offer her goodnights. She found her in her bedroom. The young girl seemed embarrassed to be alone in Athena's company, her face was flushed, and she fidgeted with the pen in her hands.

"I've just come to say goodnight," Athena said to her brightly. She noticed Neti's awkwardness but persevered.

"Kat seems better ... but you must wake me if you're at all concerned tonight. I'll keep an eye on her though."

Neti nodded. "You probably didn't need to come. I'm sorry ..."

Athena was quick to reassure her that she had done the right thing and acknowledged that, in fact, it had been a very responsible thing to do.

Neti smiled shyly as she continued to fidget with the pen. Its top shot out of her fingers and rolled under the dressing table. Diving after it, she retrieved with it the note that Rupert had written to her explaining his absence.

"Oh ..." She read it and handed it to Athena.

"There you are!" Athena said smiling. "Your uncle was thinking of you. Apparently, he did phone to say that he would be home tomorrow."

Neti seemed so waif-like and vulnerable, and Athena was moved that it was Rupert who cared for her. Although it need not be Athena's concern, she worried about what the future held now for this girl.

Already, Toby was asleep, exhausted from the excitement of his day. Athena moved to the other side of the bed and lay on top of the bedclothes, feeling embarrassed to sleep within them. Although it was not late, she was weary and quickly fell into a shallow sleep. Accustomed as she was to checking on Toby during the nights that he stayed with her, she woke regularly, listening for any sounds from Kat. On one occasion she got up and went into the lounge room. By the passage light left on for her she could see that Kat slept quietly and, by her side, on the floor, Neti lay in a sleeping bag.

Wide-awake, Athena lay back on Rupert's bed and took in the room by the lamp's glow. It was bare of curiosities, other than some craft pieces that furnished it. On the bedside table next to her, though, was a small clay sculpture of a house, apparently made by a child. Despite its imperfections it was charming with its pitched roof and crooked chimney — an ideal family home, the imperfections making it all the more endearing.

Athena, deep in thought, leaned across to her brother and gently kissed his forehead. She thought about her life and was happy with its direction — her research was fulfilling and, indeed, she loved it. She knew too that she would like to have a family, though it had not been an immediate concern. Lately, though, she was sensing gaps, as if something in her life might be missing.

She studied the clay house more closely. In a faint, child's handwriting inscribed on its little front lawn were the words:

"Uncle Rupert's house".

CHAPTER NINE

The days and nights that Rupert spent with Matthew passed all too quickly. Rupert considered staying longer but still unsettled by his conversation with Kat, decided against it.

Though Matthew had moments of lucidity, his health declined further, and he was now confined to his bed and slept for most of the time. Despite this deterioration, the doctor could not give a definite answer regarding how much time Matthew might have left. It was possible that he could remain in this state for some weeks.

On the day of his intended departure, Rupert rose early. Though he had slept in Matthew's room with him and had spent virtually every moment of his time with him, he dreaded the thought of saying goodbye.

As Rupert sat by the bed, Matthew opened his eyes.

"You're leaving," he whispered hoarsely.

"I'm coming back."

Matthew smiled weakly.

"I'll see you again, Elijah."

He closed his eyes and drifted into sleep. Rupert, swallowing against the thickness in his throat, kissed the silver-grey head and left, not daring to look back.

As he drove out the gates of the Community, he wondered if he would ever return.

The days spent with Matthew had given Rupert time to reflect on his life. He was no closer to solving his dilemmas regarding Neti and Kat, nor where he was to live, but during the days spent in the peace of the Community, Rupert felt a small thawing of his heart to his religion and, with the gentle persuasion of Matthew, to his father.

It had been too long since Rupert had visited him, but he didn't linger on the unpleasant thoughts of their last meeting; he feared he would lose the limited courage and motivation he now had. When he parked the car outside the aged care centre where his father now lived, he noticed that his hands were trembling. Would he ever lose the trepidation he had in seeing his father? he wondered but suspected he would always feel that he was still just a child in his father's eyes.

"I'm here to see Walter Brown," he told the receptionist.

She smiled. "Which one?"

"Reverend."

"And you are?"

"His son," Rupert said quickly, afraid that his name might be recorded on a blacklist.

She smiled again.

"Yes ... he's outside. I saw him being taken there only a few minutes ago."

Like Matthew, Rupert's father sat in a wheelchair in the garden, a blanket on his lap to keep out the autumn breeze. Unlike Matthew, this was not a frail man. The Reverend

Brown sat erect in his chair as if in position to command the garden.

As Rupert came up behind him, he saw the swirl of hair at the crown like his own. He wondered if his father was ever aware of it and how ludicrously vulnerable it made him appear, in spite of his rigid spine. In one sense, that swirl was an insignificant physical feature, but Rupert felt his stomach knot when he saw it — a reminder that no matter how much he might want to deny it, the two of them were linked in blood. Ross did not share this aberration, and Rupert wondered, with dread, how else he might resemble the man before him.

Careful not to startle him, Rupert moved around to face him and bent down.

"Hello Father."

The older man took him in, warily at first, and, to Rupert's great relief, smiled.

"Ross!"

Rupert's heart leapt to his throat in panic. He had been told that his father knew of Ross's death.

"No, Dad," he said, using the less formal, less used, name for his father. "I'm Rupert."

The Reverend Brown's eyes sharpened.

"What are you doing here?"

His father's eyes were fixed in a predator's stare. Rupert leaned forward and reached out to him, but he pulled away, securing his hands under the blanket.

"I don't want you here."

Flecks of white spit collected on the older man's lips.

Still squatting, Rupert rested his head in his hands and searched the ground for the confidence that was draining through his feet. His father was silent above him, and it seemed, in that moment, that the world held its breath.

Why had he come? He didn't know, but he'd felt compelled

to. Time and all that lay broken between them had done nothing, it seemed, to lessen his father's disdain. At least, Rupert thought, his father was not indifferent, and he drew some encouragement from that.

There was little that he could do, and even less that he could say. Rupert raised his head and stood up. Leaning over his father he embraced him and kissed him on the temple.

"I love you, Dad."

The older man did not flinch and remained stony and silent. But as Rupert walked away, he could feel his father's eyes follow him until he was out of view.

He would come back and try again, and it would be all right.

———

When Rupert came through the front door, everything seemed to be as he had left it. Though, to a certain degree, this was of some relief to him, he felt that it was symptomatic of the people who lived in it; as if, in dying, Ross had pushed a pause button for those who had been left behind, and they were now faced with the ever-present reminder of his absence in their lives. None of them, including Kat, was capable of getting on with the job of living. In Kat's case, Rupert suspected, she had lost her excuse for her desertion and was now floundering in her attempts to make up ground with Neti.

At the sound of the front door closing, Kat appeared from the kitchen; she seemed happy enough to see him. Some things have changed, he thought to himself, though not without suspicion. At the same time, Neti came out from the bedroom.

"You're back early," he said, smiling at her, "did you have a good time?"

"Yep."

Neti and Kat returned to the kitchen.

In his bedroom, Rupert was softly aware of a difference. Everything was in order, but he felt a strange yearning, as if for something that was lost or something he may never attain. He unpacked thoughtfully and, when he came out, his expression prompted Neti, who was heading back to her room, to speak.

"Athena ... and Tobias stayed in your room."

Rupert shook his head as if he had misheard, "What? What's that?"

Guiltily, Kat emerged from the kitchen once more, having heard Neti's admission.

"I was ill, Ru. Neti was worried and found Athena's number."

"Are you alright?" he said, seeing now that Kat was pale and drawn.

She hesitated, "We'll talk about it later?" and looked guardedly towards Neti.

Neti's voice squeezed between them.

"She's nice ... Athena, I mean."

Kat nodded.

"But how did you find her number?" Rupert said, still bewildered.

Blushing, Neti told him.

"You're very resourceful," he said with a smile.

"It's not hard to find things in *your* room," she answered him over her shoulder as she stepped lightly to her bedroom.

Rupert turned to Kat once certain that Neti was out of hearing range.

"What's wrong?"

Kat stammered a reply that she was all right. Rupert was becoming used to her evasiveness and was not prepared to go along with it. He stood silently, waiting for her to tell him more.

She was nervous, he could tell by the way she avoided

looking at him, and he saw the subtle shifting of her weight from foot to foot, as if restraining herself from fleeing.

He waited, predicting what would happen next; she would become defiant as a defence.

"I'm pregnant."

Her eyes held his, but he looked away. There was an awful feeling of reliving a moment, in this house, many years before. Back then, he had asked her if she was carrying Ross's child; a terrible question to ask of her, but Rupert was uncertain where her restlessness would take her. It was Ross's, she had said with vitriol, and Rupert suspected that therein lay the problem.

"Whose?" he asked with resignation.

She looked away.

"Guy."

He waited, and wondered in her pause, if he was supposed to know this.

"Sit down?" she said.

Rupert dropped into the armchair. Kat went immediately to her favoured position on the couch and tucked her legs in front of her like a fortress.

"I've known Guy for five years." She hesitated, as though waiting for a response, but Rupert sat silent and perplexed.

"When I first moved north ... I was very lonely and unclear as to what I should do ... I reached a very low point in my life."

Rupert resisted the temptation to reply with cynicism.

Kat continued the conversation to her fingernails, and Rupert could see that her hands were shaking.

"After a time ... a long and terrible time ... I was guided to a local Buddhist Sangha." Kat looked up and her eyes brightened at the memory but quelled when they flicked across his face. "Anyway, I met Guy there and, after a time, we began to live together ... for the last four years."

It sounded reasonable enough, but Rupert was shocked that

he knew so little about Kat's life in the years since she'd left. During the last few weeks spent in her company, not once had she told him and, he thought with some shame, neither had he asked.

"What happened?"

Kat leant back on the pillow behind her and looked at the ceiling, her hand straying to push lightly on her abdomen in what seemed to be an unconscious movement.

"Oh ... I don't know ... me, I suppose ... or, I should say," she looked at Rupert, "me, as usual? Guy is ten years younger ..."

Rupert's eyes widened at this information.

"But I got restless."

He'd thought that it was possible for people to change. It seemed that some traits are so deeply rooted that the best some can do is to prune the exterior into something that is more acceptable — to themselves and to others. In the end though, a shoot off the old root finds its way to daylight.

"Why did you come back, Kat?"

"I thought about Neti a lot. I thought that I wanted to be the mother I should have been. When I received your letter ... it seemed heaven-sent."

Rupert cringed at her words.

Kat seemed to sense his thoughts and coloured. She went on quickly, "I didn't know, when I came, that I was pregnant."

Rupert remembered the telephone conversation he had overheard. He realized now who Kat must have been talking to.

"And he knows?"

"Yes."

Rupert remembered too, that the conversation had sounded heated. It seemed that the news of Kat's condition was causing conflict. He assumed briefly, that this younger man, Guy, was not pleased with the prospect of fatherhood.

"Guy wants me to go home," Kat said, almost answering his thoughts.

Rupert was taken aback. He hadn't expected this but was also conscious of Kat's terminology. Where did she consider her home to be?

There was a pause before she continued, and she pressed again with her hand, "But I just want to get rid of it."

He should have been used to it — the smack-in-the-face remarks. When she said it, he wondered why he would ever have thought that she would think any differently. He closed his eyes against the oppressive sense of déjà-*vu*.

"I need money, Ru," she said as a natural extension to her previous statement.

He was appalled at what she was requesting, and his voice wavered as he answered her.

"I couldn't."

"*Jesus!*" Kat said through her teeth. "*What do you expect me to do?*" Her voice was rising, and her face was pale with rage.

Though he knew that Neti had gone to her room, Rupert was anxious that she not hear them. He didn't know what she already knew. He spoke softly, "Kat, please ... I can't."

"*Forget it!*" she said, loud and hot as she rose from the couch. "*I'll beg at the clinic.*" She swept passed him, knocking herself on the coffee table as she headed for her room. She looked back at him with bitterness.

"I'm not going to relent *this time*,"

In the awful silence that was left behind, Rupert heard the soft click of Neti's door closing.

She heard it, behind the door, ear cocked at the crack. She knew it too. She wanted Kat to love her, but she knew that she was unlovable. Kat must have known that, when she was pregnant with her; she must have known that the baby she was carrying wouldn't inspire love or sacrifice. Polly inspired love. Neti could see the way Polly's parents responded to her. They didn't say it all the time, "I love you," like Kat did, hollow-sounding words, but they showed it, because they got cross, like Rupert sometimes did. Kat never got cross. She got annoyed though, as if she was being asked to give a piece of herself that she didn't want to give. She had thought that Ross had loved her, but in the end, she wasn't enough to live for.

Neti thought about the letter she had found in Rupert's cupboard. She would have been five when her father had written it. Kat would have left them by then. What did Ross have to say to his brother? Was the answer there — why Kat had left? Why she found her child to be so unlovable?

She must read it. She would wait, when Rupert and Kat were out, and she'd find the answer.

Saturday mornings had a different feel to them now, Rupert thought as he got out of bed. When he was living in the College, he would rise early, as he still did, and wander down to one of the cafes in the local shopping strip. He hadn't developed the taste for coffee as, it seemed, everyone else in Melbourne had. Though the range to choose from seemed excessive, he was still able to get a good cup of tea, and he enjoyed watching the world go by. He was never aware of being lonely in those days.

These days his loneliness felt like a low-grade infection, and his old routine seemed foreign to him now. Rupert showered and dressed and considered what he might do. He had not slept well the previous night. Still astonished by the fact that Athena and Toby had spent the night in his bed, he was experiencing a range of emotions as a result. He was, firstly, so grateful to Athena for coming to Neti's aid. At the same time, he was bothered that he had not been here, although the circumstances had not allowed for much else. But what had kept him awake, apart from everything else, was the knowledge that Athena had slept here and that he had kissed her, the last time they had met. He was now highly conscious of the presence of her perfume in the room — not strong, but subtle and evasive. There were times, in the night, when he found himself drawing in long breaths to find it. When he did, he let it wash through him, but he experienced a feeling of longing — he didn't know what for, but it was both pleasant and disturbing.

As he lay there, he wondered if he was in love with Athena. Love, or, at least, emotion disguised as such, wasn't unfamiliar. In his youth he'd experienced several crushes; one, in particular, had caused him great grief when it wasn't returned. In his late teens, Rupert had a relationship for several months, but it came to an end when the friendship moved to a sexual relationship — neither was ready for the intensity of it. In the years that followed, Rupert fell in love with Marjorie, or so he'd thought. Their relationship was one of deep friendship and respect. Although it remained a platonic one, there was never a question of it becoming sexual, though Rupert would admit to himself that, once or twice, he fantasized about sharing that sort of intimacy with her. When Marjorie married, he felt nothing but joy for her, and their friendship remained as strong as before.

But there was something else in his thoughts about Athena. He didn't know her well, and so he suspected that any ideas of love would be impetuous, let alone inappropriate. She was possibly six or seven years his junior, though this was not apparent in their conversations. When he thought of her though, he felt warm, almost joyful. But he was suspicious of this feeling. Rupert had begun to recognize that he had never been a joyful person, having been content to offer up unnamed dissatisfactions to his God. Now, it seemed there was an urgency to experience joy.

He decided to go to the market. Before he left, Rupert checked that Kat was all right. She had been quiet in the night and, when he knocked on her open door to ask her if she wanted a cup of tea, she responded with a groan of annoyance. He heard Neti in her room and knocked there too, to see if she would come with him. She'd been through a difficult time with Kat, and he wanted to make up for his absence when she would have needed him. He hoped that she might even talk to him about how she was feeling.

Neti answered her door, still in her pyjamas. She didn't want to come, she said, but thanked him anyway. She wanted to know how long he would be gone. He didn't know, he said, but maybe a couple of hours.

Rupert headed for the market. He loved the atmosphere there, especially the displays of fresh produce. Travelling overseas had made him appreciate more deeply the abundance at home. The delicatessen stores especially intrigued him, and he resolved to expand his culinary knowledge to broaden the menu at home. But it was the milling of people of different ages and nations of origin that he liked most of all.

In the crisp air of these now colder mornings, he was greeted by the odour of baking bread, and the wood fires of the market cafes. With so many stalls, Rupert liked to take his time moving through them in order to find the best produce for price. He was purchasing the last items when he saw Athena ahead of him, paying for the fruit and vegetables she had just bought and that were weighing heavily in the bags she was carrying. She was dressed in the red coat that she had worn to his office on their first meeting, and her hair was tucked into a woollen hat of the same colour. He suddenly felt nervous but approached her to offer to take her bags to add to his own. She turned to him at the sound of the voice and her face brightened when she saw who it was.

Athena handed her bags to Rupert at his insistence and, although she seemed genuinely delighted to see him, there was a brief, awkward moment where both seemed to be lost for something to say.

"Would you like to join me for breakfast?" Rupert said at last, indicating with his head in the direction of one of the cafes, but noticed as he did so, that it was very crowded.

"I'd love to, but I don't think there's much room this morning. If you've finished your shopping, how about breakfast at my place?"

Rupert accepted, a little too eagerly, he thought, and they headed off to their own cars.

Athena wondered if Rupert saw through her to the guilt she felt for thinking about him too often; for thinking about him at all. Thoughts of him were now lying like underfelt to her daily routines. She had handed him her bags too readily trying to create a distraction, and now that they were with him in his car, she felt stripped; more exposed to him somehow.

Occasionally, she allowed herself to revel in the warmth she felt in thinking of him — she had done that, the night on his bed. Athena had pictured him in that room, dressing and combing his untameable swirl as he looked in the small mirror on the chest of drawers. She had imagined him too, lying on the bed, as she was, and, before long, had thought about the kiss. More often, though, she berated herself for slipping into these thoughts. She didn't know Rupert well enough, and she felt that her feelings resembled a childish crush. More significant was the futility of such emotion, and, still in the shadow of her broken engagement, she did not want to needlessly expend that energy again.

Used to analysing emotions, including her own, Athena wondered if, underlying her attraction to Rupert, was the knowledge that a relationship between them could never amount to anything. Was it safe, she wondered, to have romantic notions about him, especially now that she was going away?

She comforted herself with this thought as she parked the car and went inside to wait for him. She felt more confident now, but when Rupert knocked on the door and she saw him standing on her doorstep, his face pale and his nose red from the cold, her inner self sighed in defeat. Stepping aside for him to enter, she took in the back view of his lean frame that was slightly stooped with the weight of her bags. He has two recalcitrants in his life, she thought with a smile — Neti and that swirl of hair.

In the kitchen, Athena unpacked the shopping bags, while Rupert sat at the bench. She felt strangely comforted by his presence there.

"I must thank you," Rupert said, his voice wavering a little, "for coming to the aid of Neti and Kat."

Athena felt her face colouring at the mention of her stay, and answered him quickly, "Not at all, I didn't do much, really."

"It was a great imposition on your time, Athena ... Thank you."

Athena nodded in acceptance of his gratitude and inquired after Kat. His answer was evasive.

"I know that Kat's pregnant, Rupert," she said directly.

He seemed relieved but became agitated when she asked him what Kat planned to do. He told her what Kat had said, and how she wanted him to contribute to the termination of the pregnancy.

Athena poached eggs while she listened.

"Well, it's a difficult one," she said when he had finished.

Rupert raised his eyebrows in agreement. Athena had wondered, since that evening, what she would do if in the same predicament as Kat. She thought she knew but was also aware that circumstances can force a change of mind. She had experienced that when she knew that her mother was carrying a child with Down syndrome. Concerned for her parents and the strain on their resources — materially and emotionally — Athena had hoped that they would come to the decision to terminate the pregnancy. They didn't, and she was glad now. Equally, though, circumstances might not have led to such a happy outcome as Toby.

Rupert didn't offer any more thoughts on the subject but did ask Athena if she thought that Neti knew. She couldn't be certain, she said, but suspected that she didn't.

"Neti kept Toby busy for the evening. She was wonderful."

Rupert's face brightened and his eyes flicked in search of Athena's brother.

"He's gone home for the weekend," she said, serving up the eggs and placing a plate in front of Rupert, feeling all the while that it was a very natural thing to do.

"How's your friend, Matthew?"

Rupert's face clouded, "Ailing, but he has come to terms with dying. For his sake, I hope that it won't be long."

Athena could see in Rupert's face that, in another sense, and for his own sake, he didn't mean this at all.

There was a pause as they ate and as Athena decided whether to pursue this conversation, but Rupert spoke before her.

"Any breakthroughs in your research?"

"There may never be any," she replied, "but I hope there will be."

"This is sounding like an act of faith is involved," Rupert said mischievously and took another mouthful of his breakfast.

Athena smiled at the joke. It was in such discussions that their differences were most apparent. She knew that he liked to bait her, with good humour, and she enjoyed their interchanges.

"The answers will be found eventually, though perhaps not in our lifetimes. I do believe in a knowable universe, and I believe that we are evolving with it, and to know it."

"And when we know it?" Rupert prompted as he cut into his toast. "No more mystery?"

"I don't need the mystery," Athena responded, "I'd rather know."

"I wonder if that's what everyone will feel. I suspect that most of us need mystery in our lives."

Athena considered what he was saying while she finished the mouthful she was eating, "I don't think the concept of god will disappear, if that's what you mean?" Rupert's look was quizzical, and she continued, "There could still be a place for God."

His eyebrows shot up in surprise. Athena laughed, "Not that I'm suggesting there should be one, however," she said more seriously, "we *are* physical creatures, governed by physical laws and, if you believe, created to be that. Surely then, a creative God would enable us to know it through physical means. Perhaps, Rupert, your God whispers to you through your wiring."

Rupert was quiet as he carried his plate to the sink. Athena wondered if she was touching on a raw nerve. She knew he was struggling with his faith, and she didn't know if she was making matters worse.

He was behind her as he spoke, "When you say, everything will be known, you mean emotions ..." Rupert turned on the tap to rinse his plate, almost drowning out his next words. "Even love?" He turned off the tap.

Had she thought of something to say to fill that silence, she would have. But she couldn't, and didn't, and Athena was conscious that that little silence said too much. She tried to disguise it then with mock innocence but felt that her physiology was betraying her. She didn't turn to face him.

"Well ... there have been some indications that serotonin might have a role in the feelings of love."

She felt him move behind her and held her breath. He paused briefly and returned to sit opposite her again.

"You wear a particular perfume," he said softly.

Athena was lost for words. It wasn't so much what he had said, it was more the tension that existed between them at that moment, as if anything said now would be stretched and strained to the point of snapping. She sucked in air and took her own plate to the sink, turning the water on more forcefully than she intended.

"Something that I found out, about Matthew," Rupert continued, but had to raise his voice over the noise of the water, "He loved ... or, in fact, still loves a woman ... Clare."

"Oh?" Athena said matter-of-factly enough as she returned to her seat, though it was far from how she was feeling.

Rupert continued to tell Athena what he had learned about Matthew's past, and his own visit to Clare. She could see in his telling, that Rupert was genuinely surprised by this news and, she suspected, a little hurt that he hadn't known this about Matthew before.

"How do you feel about this?" she said, with more than simple curiosity.

Rupert thought for a moment before answering, "I was shocked at first, no doubt about it, but not disappointed. Matthew did make a choice, and one that he was ever faithful to. Having thought about it for a while, though, I wonder if he made the right choice. His love for Clare is real still, and perhaps they could have shared a wonderful life together."

As he spoke, he looked down at his hands and at the ring on his finger. At one point, when he looked up and directly into Athena's eyes, she felt like a rabbit caught in a headlight and couldn't take her eyes away.

Rupert continued, "But there's something about Matthew's simple faith — not a blind faith; I think it's been hard won. It's something beautiful to see, and somehow, when you're with him, you think it might be possible to find that too."

Athena watched him. His eyes, though sad, had a youthful look of innocence and hope. Impulsively, she reached across the bench and touched the back of his hand. He turned it over and clasped her hand in his own.

Who knows who made the first move, from their chairs, around the bench, the culprit hands still joined. Who was the first to embrace? Whose chemistry led the mutiny? Athena didn't know, didn't care at that moment — she didn't think anything much — such moments are carefree and, her deeper self already knew, that's the trouble.

Neti lay on her back in her bed, her body tense as she strained to hear if her uncle was still moving about the house.

Kat rarely woke before ten o'clock, so Neti knew that she had some time to retrieve the letter from the box in Rupert's cupboard, read it and return it, before anyone would notice. Although logic told her that it was unlikely that anyone *would* notice, the relatively simple act that she was intending had grown, in her mind, to espionage.

Why does he take forever? Fussing around before leaving, she thought. Neti thought she heard the front door close and held her breath to ensure total silence. She listened for the close of the car door, the standard three attempts to start the engine, the *putt putt* as the car took off. She held her breath again, listening for the sound of a sudden return — string-bags forgotten, or a warmer jacket needed.

Another five minutes, she thought. He'd be far enough away by then that anything forgotten would remain so.

Neti trod softly across the floorboards to her door and, opening it, cocked her ear for any sound coming from Kat's room. She usually slept with the door well open as if fearing something in that room. Neti thought of her father, that he had also slept with that same door ajar, but she knew that that was in case she needed something in the night.

It hurt her when she thought of him; memories of him bringing her a warm Milo and toast on Saturday mornings. He would come in and kiss her on her forehead. She always pretended that she was asleep, just so she could enjoy his presence there without having to speak. She would peep at him as he placed the cup and plate on the bedside table. Frequently, she knew, he had a headache from drinking the night before, but when she opened her eyes wide, he would brighten and sit down on her bed to talk.

They loved to talk, Neti and her dad. They were mates, she had thought, just sort of drifting through life together.

Neti closed her eyes and hugged her thoughts inside. They ached.

When certain that the coast was clear, she crept into Rupert's room. She didn't hesitate at the cupboard but pulled the box out quickly and began riffling through its contents looking for the letter. There seemed to be more in the box now and thought that Rupert must have placed other items in here since he had come home. She couldn't find the letter. Neti panicked. She wondered if Rupert had already guessed her plan and had taken it out of the box. He did know that she'd found Athena's telephone number in there. Neti took in a large breath and held it while she looked again; she expelled it audibly with relief, holding the letter victoriously.

Quickly, Neti replaced the box and left the room with her prize. She stopped at Kat's doorway, the letter tucked into her pyjama pants. Kat's intermittent snoring reassured Neti that she had the time she needed. Inside her room, she debated the best place to read the letter. She dragged an old armchair to face the window. On the way, she stopped at the mirror and tussled her spikes. Neti climbed into the chair, tucking her legs beneath her. With trembling hands, she pulled the letter from the envelope and spread its pages on her lap, smoothing the creases with almost exaggerated movements.

Neti hesitated before beginning. She listened again for any sound of Rupert's return, or her mother awake. She was afraid that the voice of her father would be loud in its protest at being read.

Dear Ru

I think I need to write my thoughts down and perhaps, in sending them to you, I might be able to think more clearly.

I'm sorry about the other night. Too much drink as usual. I didn't mean what I said. I would never go through with it, no matter how low I might feel. I wouldn't do that to Neti.

My poor little girl. I'm afraid, Ru, that I won't be enough for her. I love her — you know that, but how will I ever be able to compensate for the absence of her mother? Neti deserves so much more than I can give her.

Neti stared out the window and thought about her father, and how hard he tried to make up for Kat's absence, even trying to bake cakes that he inevitably burnt. They would laugh about it and eat the cakes anyway, scraping off the burnt edges and smothering the centres with cream.

She thought, too, of her thirteenth birthday, and how he had taken her to the underwear section of a department store. He thought, because she was now a teenager, that she would need a bra and dutifully handed her over to the store assistant to be measured. The woman smiled as she moved the tape measure away. You're lucky, she had said, you won't need one of these for a while. She was right, and Neti told her father this quite matter-of-factly when she emerged from the booth. She remembered that he was standing awkwardly amongst the various lingerie items and relieved by this news, grabbed her by the hand and led her out. They went to eat pancakes — triple-stacked with maple syrup and ice cream. They both felt sick that night, but had to put on a brave face together, because Rupert was coming to celebrate her birthday. He brought a big cake, with cream and icing. Neti and her dad shared a secret, pained smile when they saw that; they knew they would have to eat it.

Saddened by the memory, Neti read on.

I'm not coping without Kate, Ru. You're probably grimacing to read that, but I really did think we could make a go of it. Even Mum and Father had something, didn't they? I suppose you won't agree with that. But even the worst marriages have some comfort ... the known, the presence of the other. All the times that Kate would go away, I knew that she would come home — but now? I thought that when she knew she was pregnant, things might change, that she might want to start a family with me, but — maybe I pushed her into it. Maybe I shouldn't have insisted that she keep the baby. Then perhaps she'd still be here. But then, I wouldn't have my Neti, and I hate to think of life without her.

Kate says she doesn't love me — that she never has. I don't believe it, Ru. You remember how we were, don't you? In the early days we were happy. I know she's had some problems — the pills and all, but we could have gotten over that.

Neti thought of the time she saw Kat frantically rummaging through her bag, looking for something. When she saw Neti she gave her a suspicious look and accused her of taking 'them'. Neti didn't know what she was talking about, and she was afraid. Kat looked wild, her face was flushed, and her eyes were wide and glassy looking. She had searched through the bag again and raised a small bottle of tablets triumphantly. She didn't apologise but brushed past Neti to the kitchen. Neti didn't follow her. She could hear the running water and the clink of the glass as Kat swilled down the pills.

*I don't know what I would have done without you. I know
you're coming back to keep an eye on us. I feel guilty about that.
I know that you've found peace in the Community, and it will
be quite a different life at the College, but it will be a comfort to
know that you're here. Neti loves you and I know you love her.*

Neti picked the envelope up from the floor and studied the
address on the front. Under Rupert's name, her father had
addressed it to some place that didn't sound like an ordinary
street name and number but more like a country address —
Wattle Valley — she'd heard of it before. It sounded like the
place that Rupert had just visited to see his old friend.

She was surprised to learn that Rupert had lived elsewhere,
having only ever remembered him living at the College and
visiting often. He'd always been in her life, she had thought,
and now she realized that this hadn't been the case. It sounded
as though he had been happy where he was. She began to feel
ashamed — that she had been making life so difficult for her
uncle when, once again it seemed, he had left a life behind to
look after her.

*I'll try to keep myself together, Ru. I know I've given you some
difficult times — I've got to give up the drink before it kills me. I
owe that to Neti especially. It will be good to spend time
together, won't it? I know that Kate has tried to put a wedge
between us, but nothing can ever really separate the Terrible
Two — can it?*

Can't wait to see you. In the meantime, don't worry about us.

Your loving brother,
Ross

The letter slid from Neti's knee. She didn't attempt to catch it but got up and went to her bedside table and took out her diary. She unlocked it and took out the photograph of her mother and father taken in the hospital after her birth — the one in which she had thought that they looked like a happy family. She studied Kat's face. How was it that she had not seen it before? There was a look of misery in her mother's eyes, but a look of naïve joy in her father's. This time, Neti placed her thumb over Kat's face and focused instead on that of the man who had truly loved her.

A noise in the kitchen startled her. Neti rushed over to the letter and tried to cram it back into its envelope. Rupert must have forgotten something, she thought, or, she began to panic, he had guessed. She listened at the door. It wasn't Rupert, but Kat. Despite hushed and guarded tones, she was quite audibly talking on the telephone. Neti crept cautiously toward the kitchen, avoiding familiar and reliably squeaking floorboards. She listened near the kitchen door but couldn't determine what Kat was saying. She could hear, though, an urgency in her voice that overlay a sound of resignation. Neti guessed that her mother was talking to her boyfriend — the baby's father. She knew, of course; she had heard these conversations on the telephone before, and she had guessed, when Kat was ill. It was all confirmed when she heard Rupert and Kat talking the night before.

The baby ... She rolled it over in her mind and on her tongue. She felt some jealousy, that this baby was so close to Kat, at least physically, but remembered what she had heard last night. Kat did not want the baby and, it seems, had never wanted her either.

Suddenly, Neti felt a pang of anxiety, a need to protect this unborn child, for itself and, perhaps, for herself too. Who looked out for her when she was '*the baby*'? She knew the answer now — her father and ... Rupert, who, it seemed, looked out for many of them.

The conversation was brief. When Neti heard her mother replace the receiver with a loud click, she thought she also heard her catch the air in a gasp.

Neti could have made her escape then but was stuck to the spot; partly out of concern for Kat, but also because she recognised the winds of change, and they bore bad news. She shivered.

Kat made another call — short and sharp. It was not a personal call; Neti could tell that by the clipped and efficient way Kat spoke, the way she said goodbye. Kat opened the door and charged through, already carrying herself awkwardly, as though anticipating a future weight in her body. She stopped sharply when she saw Neti. A look of guilt flashed quickly across Kat's face, but was replaced with a shrug of her eyebrows. She paused before speaking.

"Pack some clothes, love, for warm weather. We're going to Kyogle."

Neti took a step back. She hadn't expected this one. She thought that Kat might go, had even come to expect it, but she never dreamed that she would go too.

"We have to, Neti," Kat said firmly, "there's no other choice."

The edge of bitterness in her voice was not lost on Neti. Kat continued, softer this time.

"I'm having a baby, love." She paused, her face colouring. "You'll like Guy ... He wants you to come."

Neti felt a shift in her stomach.

"What about Rupert?"

Kat stared at her and took a deep breath, its slow exit adding a dark emphasis to her reply.

"Just pack and do it quickly. T-shirts, shorts, underwear.

Your diary. Anything else you need I'll buy up there when I can."

Neti couldn't move, this time because her feet *wanted* to be rooted to the spot. She could refuse. Kat couldn't *make* her go, she thought. Her knees trembled.

She thought then of *the baby*, and what might happen to it now. Kat might be going to keep it after all, she thought, but Neti was still concerned.

"I'll come," she said directly, as if she had a choice.

CHAPTER TEN

For the moments that they held each other, Rupert was only aware of the scent of Athena's hair, of the shyness of his own lips on hers, and the absolute relief it was to hold and to be held. But as soon as there was the smallest separation between them, it seemed as if that space filled rapidly with all manner of their concerns, until they stood facing each other, the silence filled with the noise of their individual thoughts.

Rupert couldn't remember who had made the first move but suspected that he had. Athena had responded freely; he felt that in her warmth, but he felt ashamed now, because there was nothing that he could offer her. He went to speak, but she spoke before him, her eyes cast down.

"I'm leaving for America in a week."

He had known that she'd considered going but had put it to the back of his mind. Now, he was troubled to hear it confirmed. Despite his own confusion about what had just passed between them, he felt that this news was bringing an unexpected and unwelcome finality that he had not considered. A gulf lay between them, still thick with unresolved emotion. Their arms, that had still been holding each other, dropped to their sides.

"Will I see you before you go?" Rupert's heart was heavy as the inevitability of her leaving sank in.

Athena still hadn't looked up at him, and she nodded to his chest.

Rupert felt that he should go, but, at the same time, didn't want to move, afraid that the break would be irredeemable. Athena took a step back and faced him now.

"Are you okay?"

"Yes ... Are you?"

She smiled and seemed to be searching his face for reassurance.

"I think we've been impulsive," she said with a small laugh.

Rupert appreciated what she was offering as way of an excuse. Though he would agree in one sense, he could not deny that the emotion that led to it, at least on his part, was genuine.

He placed his hands on her shoulders and drew her to him. The atmosphere was less charged now, but he could not think of anything adequate to say. This time, as he touched his lips to her hair, he savoured her longer.

They parted quietly, and without a plan. Rupert took the long way home, in order to sort out his confusion and to raise his heavy heart. Away from the heightened atmosphere of Athena's presence, his thoughts slowly ordered themselves, but only into questions that he couldn't answer. Predominantly, loomed the thought of his life without her. Already he was missing her, and he wondered at how it was possible, when he had known her for such a short time.

Whether it was because his senses had been already primed, Rupert felt that something was amiss when he pulled into the drive. Though there was nothing apparent, the house, if it was to have a character, seemed oddly silent, even glum.

He entered with a sense of foreboding; everything about this day so far having pointed to its unhappy end.

Inside, too, he felt a disturbance and looked around for concrete evidence of it. Kat's door appeared to have been flung open. Neti's stood ajar, and he knocked and entered into the room's silence. Clothing spilled forlornly from half-closed drawers, the wardrobe doors had been left open and the bed roughly made. On any given day, this room could appear the same, but there was not the usual languid feeling, but rather one of urgency, that propelled Rupert into Kat's room. It was clean and ordered, unnervingly so, as if in the tucking of the blankets, the straightening of the quilt, she had made a statement of closure.

Afraid of what they might reveal, he opened the drawers of the dresser — they were empty, but for a roll of rough cloth. He recognized the chaos of coloured threads on its exposed side and unravelled it to expose the conversely ordered and precise needlework, its simple House Blessing, half finished.

Rupert returned quickly to Neti's room, looking for, and, at the same time, afraid to find, confirmation of his thoughts. He noticed the armchair turned to the window and, as he distractedly returned it to its usual position, saw the open pages of a letter on the floor. He picked it up, noticing firstly its yellowing, and then, with a start, the idiosyncrasies of his brother's hand. His eyes scanned the pages, and he winced at the echo of the voice contained in the words.

"... Maybe I shouldn't have insisted that she keep the baby. Then perhaps she'd still be here ..."

Rupert cursed himself for his carelessness in leaving such painful reminders of Neti's history within her reach and dreaded to think how the reading of this letter might have affected her current state of mind. He reread the offending lines and thought of Kat. He could not deny the twinge of guilt he found in these words.

Rupert folded the letter thoughtfully and replaced it in the envelope Neti had discarded. He was bewildered and uncertain what he should do. Polly, he thought, Neti's friend. She might know something. In the kitchen he rang Polly's number, which was now entrusted to his memory. Polly answered but was surprised and concerned to learn that Neti and her mother may have left. She didn't know anything, she said, and asked Rupert to call her again when he discovered where Neti was.

His agitation rising, Rupert recalled his most recent conversation with Kat. She could be at the Clinic, he thought, but this didn't seem to be likely. Why would she take Neti? Why would she take all her clothing? He thought then of the baby's father, Guy. Perhaps they were headed for Queensland.

Rupert looked for signs of a number written on scraps of paper near the telephone but realized that Kat would already know it. There was nothing left in her room to give a clue. He remembered, then, the telephone bill. One had arrived since Kat had come home; she'd simply handed it to him to look after. In his bedroom, Rupert looked for it in the crude file he'd begun when he first came here. A rectangular box, with cards slotted in to make appropriate sections for the arriving bills, including the invoice for Ross's funeral. It had struck him, when he had filed that one, that his simple box was a representation of family life of sorts — school fees, medical bills and certificates that announced the arrival and departure of its members.

He retrieved the two telephone bills and selected one for its date of issue. Only one long distance number was recorded but repeated several times. He hadn't noticed this before. Rupert took it to the kitchen and dialled the number. After several rings, a male voice answered, identifying himself as Guy.

Likewise, Rupert introduced himself by name. There was a pause at the other end.

"Yes, Rupert. You're Kat's brother-in-law?"

Rupert's hopes raised. He sensed from Guy's tone that he knew something and asked him immediately if he knew where Neti and Kat might be.

"On their way here," he said matter-of-factly and with a terseness that held a warning note.

Rupert wished that he could do something to stop them. If Kat had decided to return to Queensland, that was one thing, but Rupert wasn't convinced that it would be Neti's choice to go. Despite the difficulties the preceding weeks had held for her, this was still her home. He could not imagine her leaving her best friend without a goodbye. He voiced this concern.

"She'll be happier here," Guy answered.

Rupert's reply was immediate, "But this is her home."

There was a pause before Guy spoke, more softly this time, "I think you should get used to the idea, Rupert. No doubt you know, Kat is pregnant, and Neti will be part of a real family."

A real family. The terminology hurt. Rupert knew that there was some logic in what Guy was saying. Perhaps Neti *did* want this, even needed it. Perhaps this stranger at the other end of the telephone was in a position to offer her more than he could. The morning with Athena nudged into Rupert's conscious thought, compounding his inability to provide a real family life for Neti.

Part of him, though, was still unconvinced. He needed to hear it from Neti, that she wanted to be there, before he could truly accept it. Rupert confirmed when Guy was expecting them.

"Please, ask Neti to call me when she arrives," he said.

Softer still, Guy agreed.

Rupert hadn't long put down the telephone receiver, when

there was a knock at the door. His blood pumped faster, thinking that, perhaps, Kat and Neti had changed their minds. He opened the door.

"Marjorie!"

"You seem to be disappointed," she said, laughing, and then, more seriously, "what's wrong?"

He invited her in and, on the way to the kitchen, related all that had happened, at least since he had returned home.

Marjorie listened silently, and Rupert was grateful that, when he had finished, she didn't say that it was for the best. If he was convinced that this was true, he would accept it, for Neti's sake, but he didn't want her to go, because he would miss her, and he loved her. Neti was also the only link that Rupert had to Ross, and he was certain that his brother would not want this new living arrangement.

Marjorie stroked Rupert's hand.

"I know that you're hurting, Ru. Give it some time. Wait to hear from Neti. You'll know if she's happy, and, if she is, you *will* have to adjust to it.

"And if not?"

"You'll know what to do. You have a good and loving heart — listen to it."

They sat together, sharing the comfort that small talk between friends can give. Marjorie came to the point of her visit.

"It's been four weeks, already. I haven't called you, to see if you needed more time. Are you ready to come back to work?"

Rupert was surprised that the time had passed so quickly and regretted that he hadn't called her. He apologized and considered her offer.

"If Neti doesn't come home, I can't see the point of staying here. I'd like to come back, however ..." He paused because he felt that little had changed in his feelings, or lack of, for his religion.

Marjorie seemed to sense what he was about to say, and cut in, "We'll give that time too. I didn't imagine that you would've had a change of heart so soon." She smiled. "We'll cope. Just don't voice your doubts too loudly."

Rupert returned the smile, but with gratitude for her understanding. His duties as Chaplain, however, could not be so easily feigned. He discussed this concern with her. She suggested that Rupert carry out some lighter duties, perhaps the occasional Mass, if his replacement was willing to stay on.

Aware of the efforts that Marjorie had made on his behalf, including adding his classes to her own teaching load, Rupert agreed. He walked her to her car, ever grateful for the comfort he found in their friendship.

That night, Rupert ate a light meal in front of the fire, surrounded by the unfamiliar silence of the house. Although there were days when all three of them would move quietly around each other, the house hummed quietly with their presence. Now, it seemed, the silence was deafening.

Rupert considered the events that had taken place; there were so many, that he almost found it hard to believe that they fitted into just one day. It seemed to him that, no matter which way he looked at them, he handled situations poorly. There were no happy outcomes of this day, unless he could be certain that Neti was, indeed, happy — but he would have to wait a day to know. He stared at the small flames, wishing they could offer him some solace, but they danced about the logs oblivious to him.

He addressed the silence.

Where are you now?

I don't know what to do.

There was no answer. He didn't expect it. But this was his

olive branch, held out to the God he felt had abandoned him. And though Rupert was still met by that silence, he no longer felt completely alone.

The next day, Sunday, was spent in anticipation of Neti's call in the evening. Rupert tidied the house, though it didn't need it, but in some way, he felt that he was preparing, in case she wanted to come home.

Every now and then, his thoughts would drift to Athena. He wanted to call her, and picked up the telephone on two occasions, but decided against it. He thought that perhaps he should wait for her to call but was afraid that she wouldn't. In the end, he spent the day quietly, without contact with anyone, yet feeling a little more at peace than he had in a while. As evening came, he turned his mind to returning to work the following day, while he waited to hear from Neti.

By eight thirty that night, there was still no word from her. Rupert knew that they were expected to arrive earlier, in the afternoon, but had given them time to settle in. He waited a further half hour, and when there was still no word, he decided to ring.

Guy answered, sounding irritated, as if having been interrupted. He didn't offer pleasantries but left the telephone to call Neti. Rupert strained to hear tell-tale sounds of Guy's and Neti's early relationship but heard nothing.

Unexpectedly, it was Kat's terse voice that met him from the other end.

"Yes, Rupert?"

Her tone caused him to feel guilty, although he felt quite justified in calling. Rupert was certain that she was not inclined to discuss this latest move and asked to speak to Neti.

"She's tired, Ru ... and doesn't want to talk to you. I really think it's best if you don't call for a while, so that we can get on with being a family."

Rupert was stunned and barely stammered a reply, which Kat cut across quickly.

"We're not coming back." She hesitated as if considering what she was about to say. "I think you should sell the house, Ru. It would be in Neti's interest, after all."

Rupert didn't know whether the sinister note to Kat's remark was real or whether he had just come to think of her negatively. In one sense, he had no argument against what Kat was asking. Neti was the sole beneficiary of Ross's will. If she wasn't coming home, though he was not yet convinced of this, then the money from the sale of the house would ensure her education and comfort. But it was too early to take this step; he needed to speak to Neti. Almost as soon as he raised an objection, Rupert guessed how Kat would choose to interpret it.

"You have no claim to the house," she felt the need to remind him, "and you *can* go back to the College."

Rupert tried to reason with her, but Kat became belligerent and refused to listen to him.

"You can thank *yourself* that we've gone, Ru. It's so important to you that I keep this baby, that Neti has a normal family life, well, that's what I'm doing. I don't need your advice, nor your interference."

Kat hung up the telephone before he could reply. Rupert stood with the receiver still in his hand, barely able to digest what had been said and the awful implication that he was not going to be able to speak to Neti at all.

That night, as, once again, he sat alone by the fire, Rupert slowly turned the heavy pages of the photograph album that Ross and Neti had kept, dating back ten years to the beginning of their life without Kat. Rupert had kept it in his bedroom since she had come back. He could say that he kept it from Kat, so that she wouldn't feel hurt about the years she had missed with Neti, but Rupert knew that his intention was never that honourable. He felt that Kat didn't deserve to see it; that he didn't want her to have any part in the life that Ross and Neti, and he, had shared.

He chose his favourite photograph of Ross, taken at the beach. It was a close-up, and a healthy, and apparently happy, Ross was looking over his shoulder towards Neti, the photographer. There was an angle to the shot, and Rupert, who was present at the time, remembered that Neti was ten, the camera a Christmas present that he had given her. Everything had held interest for her to photograph, but she had not yet mastered the angle and distance for the lens. Rupert remembered that the three of them had gone to the Pharmacy to pick up the first developed roll of film. Neti was so excited she was shaking. Only five of the twenty-four photographs were clear — including this one. His memory was clear about that day, as he and his brother sat on the beach, watching Neti swim.

If anything ever happens to me, Ross had said to him, I want you to look after her.

Rupert had made light of it, initially because he feared the prophecy of those words, but Ross had asked him for his promise. Rupert gave it to him.

He stared at the photograph, filled with the sense of having failed his brother, but building resolve that he would honour his promise. He knew that Ross would want Neti to be happy. If that meant that her happiness came through Kat, Rupert would accept that. But if there was any indication that this was not the case, he resolved to bring Neti home.

CHAPTER ELEVEN

Though it had only been a four-week absence from work, Rupert felt that it had been much longer — Kat's return, Matthew's imminent death, making some peace with his father, Neti gone and then, Athena; her presence had made all the difference to him during this time, and soon she would also leave.

Seated at his desk in his office, Rupert turned to the window and took in the long familiar view. The early morning light gave clarity to the silver birch trees and the sandstone wall of the building. The sporting oval, freshly mown and moist from the previous night, glowed in the sun. He had witnessed many moods of nature through this window, though, he expected his own moods probably coloured his interpretations. He viewed today with some optimism. Though Neti was gone, his resolve the night before had buoyed him. He would do everything he could do to ensure her happiness, whether she was here or afar, and he had felt a low spark of hope return.

For the next few days, Rupert worked long hours preparing for classes in the next week and catching up on correspondence. He now found some comfort in the absorption and the predictability of his day, and even looked forward to meeting with students again. He had always enjoyed the enthusiastic and the challenging students, and he felt a renewed commitment to them. Despite his own questions about aspects of theology, he would do his best to foster constructive discussion. He was less certain, though, about fulfilling his duties as priest, which required a far more intimate and genuine appreciation of his religion. He decided that the best course of action was simply to wait and see.

He had been greeted warmly by his colleagues as he came across them one by one. The theology department was not a large one, nor was there much movement amongst the staff. Rupert knew these people well, though he knew only Marjorie intimately. But he found comfort in their company and seemed to be more aware that each of them would have their own story to tell. He wondered if he had ever listened to any of them enough. Rather than avoiding them all, as he had done in the weeks after Ross's death, Rupert made sure that he went to the staff room during his breaks and sat with anyone that he found there.

He had still not heard from Neti and had to check himself on several occasions when he picked up the telephone to call her. Rupert sought Marjorie's advice and she recommended that he speak to Ross's solicitor regarding the possible sale of the house. He did so and was advised to wait. Though Neti was, indeed, the beneficiary, Rupert was executor and would be the one to make the decision when to sell, and what to do with the proceeds. Though he wanted to ensure that Neti was well looked after, Rupert was reassured that Kat had no claim to the assets left to Neti by her father.

The soles of Neti's feet burned, like roots that had been ripped from the ground. Her young back ached as she struggled with the awkwardly packed luggage — her own, and much of Kat's.

There was no money for a taxi and so mother and daughter hurried along side streets to the tram, Kat in the lead carrying her body and womb heavily, as though separate weights.

Only once, when they were settled on the tram, did Kat acknowledge her daughter's presence.

"Okay?"

Neti nodded.

Kat closed her eyes and Neti studied her face, then her belly, trying to imagine what it must feel like to have someone wrapped up inside you. She closed her eyes to picture it, but the concept was too alien for her immature body.

As the tram clicked its way toward Southern Cross Station, Neti sensed the increasing tautness of her connection with all she knew — her home, Ross, Rupert and Polly. She vaguely wondered how Kat would afford tickets for the train, and though this thought could have given her some hope, a strange foreboding quelled it. Though her world was about to change, Neti was mute, and Kat seemed indifferent to her presence anyway.

With heavy heart and burning feet, Neti juggled the luggage behind her mother at the ticket counter. Kat said something to the woman sitting behind it who, after a quick scan of the computer screen, produced two tickets.

Neti was not surprised. She could almost hear the snap as her lifeline gave way.

"Next lesson, we'll tackle the concept of Trinity."

Rupert smiled at the raised eyebrows and the sound of a soft whistle through someone's teeth.

This class of second year students was presenting a challenge — lively debates and a wider range of beliefs than he had experienced before. He enjoyed them and felt alive in their presence. Rupert doubted that they could know that; they were there for their own sakes, as they should be, extracting and discarding what they could to reshape into their own philosophies. Did they ever wonder that their source could dry up? Many thought it would, as was apparent when he met past students and the inevitable question was, "Are you *still* there?" with a look of genuine bemusement on their faces. What they couldn't know, was that they had provided the renewal.

It happened in the obvious ways, the brilliant student who sometimes stopped him in his tracks and made him rethink a theory; the reluctant student who was won over to the subject and developed a love for it that had matched his own. But often it was in the unexpected ways — the academically weak student with the brilliant spirit, in danger of being overlooked, who wrote from the heart and, after he'd waded through the incorrect use of terms, the misconceptions of theories, he would find a moment of insight, that made him want to weep for the simple truths expressed.

Rupert was surprised at how much he was enjoying teaching again. Throughout the black weeks that followed Ross's death, he'd thought that he had lost all motivation. The subject material still caused him some difficulty, but he was less bothered by it now; he was able to give his voice to the theology, even defend it at times, but it was as though he was disconnected from it.

Today, though, was to be more testing. Michael, his replacement as Chaplain, was ill and Marjorie had asked Rupert to fill in. She knew that she was asking a lot of him, but there was little else she could do, since the responsibility had fallen to the theology faculty. A Catholic mass was offered once a week for the students; the number attending had been pleasing, and Marjorie knew that this was a direct result of Rupert's influence.

That afternoon in the chapel, Rupert dressed slowly for the mass, taking in the vestry as if for the first time. Had he never studied it before? The paint-chipped walls, the highly polished oak benches and cupboards. He knelt to open one: candles, matches, a gold-plated chalice, bowls and candlesticks were all placed in an order. As he stood up, he caught the scent of lemon in the polish of the bench.

This was Lorna's domain. A widow in her sixties who lived locally, Lorna came in twice a week to clean the chapel and to prepare it for the weekly mass. Rupert knew that she came in more often than that. He had seen her, from his office window, unlocking the side door and slipping in on most other days of the week, as if conducting a clandestine affair. She didn't stay long enough to be cleaning, just long enough, he suspected, to make contact with her god in the silence.

A clipped end of a flower stem lay in a drop of water on the sink, and Rupert was aware of the smell of the recent presence of flowers that would now be adorning the altar. The spartan vestry was in stark contrast to the altar that it dressed, but its simplicity held a sense of Lorna's reverence, and Rupert decided that he preferred it in here.

As he made the final adjustments to the vestment, Rupert could hear the shuffling of the congregation. He stepped out to the presence of, perhaps, sixty, many of the faces familiar and some well-known, but most seemed to have a look of expectation. It was too soon for him, and he was suddenly very anxious that he would lose his way.

Best not to think too much, he said to himself, and entrusted his performance to memory.

He was exhausted when he arrived home but went straight to the answering machine he'd recently bought and installed. One message, not Neti, but Dominic from the Community. He would call back he said. Rupert's heart sank. The message had been left only ten minutes before. Rupert returned it immediately, his hand shaking as he pressed the numbers; he already knew what was coming.

Dominic's tone was a mixture of sorrow and apology. As if outside himself, Rupert was aware that the words he had dreaded did not shake him to the core, as he had expected.

Matthew had died while Rupert had been celebrating the Mass. He wished now that he had tried harder to see its meaning.

"The doctor is with him now," continued Dominic to the silence that met him. "It's straight forward enough. The funeral will be tomorrow."

Rupert cleared his throat.

"I'll come tonight."

When Rupert let his thoughts wander, he could feel a cold stone of sorrow radiate through him. He dreaded it but knew that it would come. At the same time though, he was somewhat surprised at the recognition that this was a return, rather than a continuance, of a grief that had begun with Ross's death. Something was happening to him. Despite what now seemed to be a steady stream of loss in his life, he didn't feel empty.

Was the world aware of Matthew's passing? he wondered. It seemed to him that passing cars were muffled and cows stood with their heads bowed, watching him pass. Death was a common denominator, he thought, and with it he felt a compassion for all who had lost a loved one, and for all who would.

Dominic greeted Rupert with sympathetic warmth, and both men walked immediately to where Matthew lay.

Though he responded automatically and pleasantly to Dominic's well-meaning small-talk, Rupert was firmly fixed in the acute present, so much so that his vision seemed keener, and the pebbles of the path appeared to rise to meet him as he walked. Before entering Matthew's room, he took in a gasp of air, as if all breath would be suspended once inside.

Barely looking at the body in the bed, Rupert sat down beside it. He was aware of Dominic's presence behind him and the small bow of reverence as he left the room, quietly closing the door behind him.

Rupert forced himself to look on the face of his friend and let out that breath in relief when he saw his peaceful countenance. Matthew looked younger than he had only two weeks earlier. Though bleached in death there was still a decided 'Matthewness' about the body. This had not been Rupert's experience with Ross, nor his mother. Rupert had felt then that the body was indeed just a shell, and that the person he knew and loved, no longer dwelt there. In his mother's case, it had been a relief to him, and to her, he suspected, that she had escaped the body she'd worn like a rusty shackle. For Ross, though, Rupert remembered his own bewilderment, his certainty that his brother was no longer there and the overwhelming despair that Ross was lost to him forever.

Not so with Matthew. It seemed to Rupert that, in Matthew's last breath, he had met with his god, and the pleasure of recognition had set into his face. This was not the result of Matthew's vocation but of his absolute faith. Rupert had witnessed the death-countenance of several of his fellow Religious. He had seen there, too, expressions such as Matthew's, but also of agony, of what appeared to be indifference, and, on one occasion, of disappointment.

Rupert rested his own hand on the shrouded one of Matthew's and felt the cold of him. He reached under the sheet and brought the hand to the surface to cup it in the warmth of his own, running his thumb along the veins that were not so prominent now. He looked around the room. It was as he had last seen it. On the bedside table lay Matthew's Bible, a box of tissues, an open packet of mints, though now the photograph of Clare was visible and rested on the edge of the table, closest to the bed. But it seemed too, that that the room had paused in its own slow decay, to consider the passing of its longest occupant.

Contentedly enough, Rupert sat, sipping memories offered by Matthew's presence. He remembered that he had not sat like this with his own brother, being too shattered, too dismayed by the sight of him. He now felt a terrible sense of guilt that he had abandoned Ross, that he had not shared his brother's death as he had his life. He wished now that he had held him, but it was too late. There was nothing left of Ross — his ashes scattered to the wind. Nothing, but memories, and Neti.

Rupert leaned across the bed and gently hooked his arms behind the body, embracing Matthew for the last time.

CHAPTER TWELVE

P acking is definitely not my strong point. Athena looked in bewilderment at the assortment of clothes on the bed. It would be Spring in Pennsylvania, that would mean the need for clothing for at least two seasons.

She had to make a decision — what was to stay and what was to go. This thought, like every second one of late, delivered her immediately to thoughts of Rupert.

The events of their last meeting had been relived in her mind over and over, unintentionally and, she decided, unwillingly. She felt as if she was not in control of her thoughts and that she could no longer stand outside herself to view her feelings in an attempt to be objective and scientific. What neurotransmitter was responsible for these thoughts of him, which were triggered by normally unrelated stimuli? The scent of a particular after-shave? Yet she was certain that Rupert did not wear one at all. A particular melody? Though she couldn't recall having heard music in his presence. But stranger still, Athena thought with a smile, was that her colleague, Bob, seemed to suddenly resemble Rupert in that his nose was also hawkish, and his eyes soft. She was conscious that, when speaking to Bob of late, she would take him in more intensely than before, and worried that she may have made him feel uncomfortable.

Not foreign to love's emotion, Athena was perplexed by its audacity. It seemed to be making her behave in unprecedented ways.

Two days ago, she'd been undecided whether she should call Rupert, to assure him that she was all right and to determine how he was feeling. Worried that such a call might now be inappropriate, she rang his faculty office instead and left a message, giving him the option of returning her call if he wanted. She was told that he was celebrating Mass in the college chapel.

What had made her go there? Curiosity? A desire to see him? Or, she felt ashamed to consider it, did she go to assess her competition?

She had slipped into the rear of the fullest pew, her hair tied up, inconspicuously dressed, and had waited. When he had entered, Athena sucked in her breath at the sight of him. He was dressed ... gloriously, for this love that he was denying.

Discreetly, she had slipped out the side door, her heart heavy.

Athena winced at the memory of it and sat heavily on the bed.

"Thenie ... you in there?"

Toby's happy, piping voice entered the room ahead of him. It never failed to make Athena smile.

Breathless and flushed, Toby found his sister sitting on the bed. He looked disapprovingly at the suitcase and clothes and cleared a space beside her. He sat, and he sighed heavily.

Athena was becoming used to Toby's tactics to make her feel guilty and didn't need any assistance in this regard. She'd spent several nights consoling him, and afterwards, herself. Her parents had implored her not to change her mind for her brother's or their sakes; it was too good an opportunity for her, they'd said, and she deserved it. But leaving was proving to be much harder than she had thought. It was a wonderful opportunity and, if she denied it, she may well regret it.

"Where's Rupert, Thenie?"

The question jolted her, as if her previous thoughts had become apparent to her brother.

"At work, I suppose." Athena tried to sound nonchalant but didn't look at him.

Toby's fifteen years of dependence had contributed to his being particularly astute in assessing the emotions and moods of others, sometimes before they were aware of them themselves. Athena was not going to give him fuel for this fire.

"I love Rupert," he said, cagily.

Athena turned to him quickly, tickling him until he begged her, through joyful screams, to stop.

"Do you indeed?" she said close to his chuckling face.

"Come on," she said standing with authority, "help me choose what to take."

Toby looked with disdain at the clothes on the bed.

"They're all ugly. You'll have to buy new ones."

Athena groaned with exasperation, and with some admiration, at this new attempt to delay her.

CHAPTER THIRTEEN

For the second time in as many days, Rupert dressed for the Mass. He was as slow as he had been the previous day, but this time, he deliberately and carefully tied the vestments in honour of Matthew.

Rupert wondered what his father would have thought when he dressed as a priest. He remembered how in awe of him he had been when he saw him in his vestments and had believed that his father was blessed. When was it that Rupert's awe was replaced with contempt? Ross had never revered their father; he'd seen through him all along. Yet, ironically, it was Ross who had shown him the greater compassion.

Rupert remembered, with love, this characteristic that marked his brother. Ross was full of failings, but he was generous in his compassion and understanding of them in others; a virtue that Rupert was still to learn.

He brought his attention back to the present and his purpose here. This time, he would say the words of the Mass and would remember their significance to the man whose life, and death, he was about to celebrate. That alone, was reason enough.

As he looked out to the congregation, composed almost entirely of community members, Rupert thought of the commitment of each person present. Was it easier to maintain faith when in the company of like minds? Rupert knew these people would hold a diversity of viewpoints about any topic, as in any other group brought together. But they had each made a commitment to God, and it was this, with all the failings that accompanied that commitment, that bonded them together.

He remembered well the wonderful times spent here in his youth. He remembered, too, when he felt he had outgrown it. And yet, he could feel the power of it even now, that intangible faith regarded too commonly now as obsolete. This world, his world, was a dying one, belittled and condemned by a different world now marching to a hyperactive drum of progress.

Rupert stared at the coffin of his mentor and friend as the Creed was read.

I believe ...

He formed the words of the prayer so well known to him now, but his thoughts wandered.

What do I believe now?

I believe in the purity and integrity of Matthew's faith.

I believe in the beauty of the human struggle.

Who suffered, died and was buried ...

For our sakes ...

I believe in the healing power of love.

CHAPTER FOURTEEN

Neti rested her head on the metal rim of the window, cooling her thoughts. She kept time on her knee with the beat of the train; no clickety-click, this was rap. She mentally repeated the words that had arisen in time with the rhythm.

"I was here, I was there, but I gotta go home
I was here, I was there, but I gotta go home
I was here, I was there ..."

With her forehead now on the glass, she shifted her line of vision from the heady blur of the tracks to the slow passage of the horizon and back again. She felt that her life was more like the tracks: racing past her with little she could focus on. It hadn't always been like that. When her dad was alive, she'd thought she could see past, present and envisage the future, but that had all changed in a single afternoon. How could so much change with one sentence? She wished she could go back, to change all events leading to Ross's death, and the words uttered by her uncle that had altered her life forever.

Neti rummaged through her shoulder-bag, looking for the

other half of the chocolate bar that lay like a crime in the bottom. She'd bought it before boarding the train with money she'd stolen from Kat that morning. She wondered if Kat had discovered it yet, and her stomach lurched at the thought of what she had done.

The past few weeks had seemed like a strange dream — the long journey to the north of New South Wales in the sole company of her mother who hardly spoke for the entire journey, meeting Guy. She'd liked him enough ... for a stranger. When they'd finally arrived, hot and exhausted from the trip and the warmer climate, Guy had greeted them with obvious relief to see Kat and seemed to be genuine in his warmth when introduced to Neti. He'd been different to what she'd expected — shorter, rounder; she wondered why she would have thought of him as being tall with long facial features. He'd tried very hard over the next few days to make them both as comfortable as possible, and Neti felt, with some relief, that he was looking forward to the arrival of the baby.

Despite Guy's efforts, it seemed that nothing would make Kat happy, and within days they were arguing. Neti had to remind herself that Kat had lived in this place, in this life, for ten years without her. Neti felt that she could no longer relate to this woman as being her mother. It was as if, away from the home Neti had known with her father, and away from her uncle, everything was out of context. The climate, the styles of houses that dotted the bushland in which they were living, were all foreign to her. She felt that she could no longer relate to herself.

The previous night, Guy and Kat had argued again. It seemed that there was nothing in particular that they argued about, but Guy would become exasperated with Kat's restlessness. He could have attributed it to her pregnancy, but there was a look in his eye, of fear, that suggested to Neti that he'd seen this many times before and knew where it could lead. Much as Neti wanted to think the best of her own mother, she suspected it would be Kat to blame for the possible failure of her relationship with Guy. When she thought this, she worried anew for the child that was to be born.

Neti stayed in her bedroom when they argued. It wasn't loud or violent, but it had an ominous tone that suggested that Neti's life might suddenly take another turn she wasn't prepared for. She was homesick and thought constantly of her own, beloved bedroom that was full of who she was. Ross was no longer in that house, but he wasn't here either. At least at home, she knew where to locate her grief.

Neti thought, too, of Rupert, and was overwhelmed at times with how much she missed him. Distance had made her realise how badly she had treated him and how gently he had tolerated her. Now, away from him, she was filled with the memories of all that he had done for her when she was a child and was struck with the realisation of what he had been sacrificing to take care of her. She was afraid for him, her kind and loving uncle, and became tearful when she thought of him sitting, at night, in that home alone. For the first time, Neti wondered how he was coping with the loss of his brother. Twice she had tried to call him but found that there was a lock on the telephone that prevented her from ringing interstate. As she lay on her bed, surrounded by an alien room and listening to the tension between Kat and Guy, Neti resolved to leave the next day and quietly packed her shoulder-bag.

As usual, the next morning, her mother was sleeping late. When Guy had gone out, Neti used the opportunity to take the money she'd seen in Kat's hand the previous day from her bag. She walked to the bus stop, keeping close to the vegetation along the road, and as soon as she heard a car, would hide herself until it had gone. For the entire half hour's bus journey, her spine tingled as if she was being chased, and she kept looking over her shoulder expecting to see Guy's car chasing the bus.

This feeling didn't leave her when she got to the railway station. Neti paid for her ticket to Melbourne and was relieved to see that the woman selling tickets wasn't the least suspicious of her. There would be an hour's wait until she could board, the woman said in monotone. Neti hid in the women's toilet.

With just a few minutes to spare before boarding, she dashed to the public telephone box to call Rupert. The unfamiliar voice of the answering machine startled her, and she hung up immediately. She purchased the chocolate bar and boarded the train, trying not to draw any attention to herself.

It was only when the train finally pulled out of the station and was travelling fast enough to outrun a car that Neti let out a long-held breath.

CHAPTER FIFTEEN

R upert felt frayed. The house, he thought as he pulled into the drive, was looking as though its fibre was unwinding. He wondered if he, and the house, would unravel together into indistinguishable threads. He thought of the back of Kat's tapestry. The garden, never a priority for Ross, looked more chaotic and neglected despite Rupert's efforts, than it had in its previous rambling state.

The drive home from Matthew's funeral had provided him with unwelcome, though necessary, time to consider his life. What gave meaning to it now that most of its significant members had left or were about to leave? He was no closer to answering the question, but Rupert could feel an urgency grow when he thought of Athena's imminent departure. He'd not had an opportunity to call on her since their last meeting, although it had weighed heavily in his heart since.

The interior of the house greeted him forlornly with a musty smell that he had not noticed before. It reminded him of houses rented by students he had visited, and seemed to symbolize transience, as if those who resided did not stay long enough to mask the house's smell with their own.

Without hesitation, and still carrying his overnight bag, Rupert checked the answering machine. There had been one call. His heart leapt that it might have been Neti, but the impersonal beep of an unrecorded message told him only that the call had been recorded at 10:00 a.m. the previous morning. He wondered then if it had been Athena saying goodbye. This, at least, provided him with an excuse to call her. He put his bag down and dialled her number before he could change his mind.

"Hello, Athena speaking."

The quick response took him briefly by surprise. He identified himself in a blurt.

There was a small, but inevitable thick silence between them. Rupert asked Athena if she'd called; she said she hadn't, but then remembered that she had called the College.

He tried to interpret her tone. It was friendly, but there was a tension in it. When he permitted thoughts of their last meeting, he knew that the tension was justified.

"I suppose you're packed and ready to go," he said, trying to sound light-hearted.

"I would be," she said with a small laugh, "but Toby keeps hindering my progress."

Three cheers for Toby, Rupert thought, but asked, instead, how he was.

"He's well, though seems to come down suddenly with an inexplicable condition whenever I talk about the trip."

From the guarded but amused sound of Athena's voice, Rupert suspected that Toby was with her. His thoughts were confirmed when he heard the boy yell a greeting to him in the background.

With mock exasperation, his sister continued, "He's very keen to see you, Rupert."

Without delay, and surprising himself, Rupert offered to visit. He genuinely wanted to see Toby but knew that this wasn't his only motivation. He explained to Athena that he had only just come in, and the nature of his recent trip was revealed.

"No don't come," Athena said suddenly, "we'll come to you ... if that's all right?"

Rupert wondered if Athena heard his sigh of relief.

Toby was delighted to be visiting Rupert. As they approached the front door, Athena leaned toward her brother and reminded him to be on his best behaviour. Rupert might be sad, she told him. He looked intently at the ground. When Athena had finished, he picked up a wilted flower lying on the path. "This's a dead flower isn'it Thenie? Things die, don'they?"

"Yes." Athena smoothed her brother's head with an affectionate hand and led him to the door. She was aware of the poignancy of the moment, when a child discovers death; she had had this discussion with Toby not so long ago. How she wished that his life could remain innocent and unaware of life's harsher truths. She knew it wasn't possible, nor, in the end, desirable, but it seemed that, since her brother had learned of death, there had been a subtle change in him. It was a maturing of sorts, but Athena worried that Toby might never be mentally equipped to put death into its natural context.

And have you? she thought to herself. Watching Toby consider the flower, she wondered if he had a better grasp of some things in life than she ever would. There were no surprises with Toby, no pretensions or complications. Life seemed to be straightforward to him. She wished, especially at this moment, that she could say the same.

She knocked on the front door. My knees are trembling, she thought with dismay, and stood rigidly. Athena looked at her brother for a distraction and some moral support. He met his sister's gaze with his own, and each gave the other a knowing, loving smile. Athena wondered at that moment more intensely, how she was ever going to leave him.

The other key figure in her current life dilemma opened the door. Rupert greeted her, too, with a smile. It was not the one of long familiarity, as Toby's, but the rudiments were there. She reminded herself that it would be potential unrealised.

The thought was broken by Toby leaping in front of her and rushing into Rupert's arms. Toby was flushed with excitement and yelled his hello. Rupert, caught up in the moment, yelled his back. Toby would not let him go and almost dragged Rupert ahead to the lounge room. Athena followed on behind, amused and bemused by her brother's antics. She was grateful to him for breaking the ice and wondered briefly if Toby had planned it. Perhaps she should reconsider his innocence, she thought with amusement.

Rupert had already set out some of the games that Toby had enjoyed with Neti. Releasing his grip on Rupert, he headed to them immediately.

Athena was aware that, other than the smile at the door, Rupert had not really looked at her, and wondered if he was uncomfortable with her presence there. With genuine warmth, though, he invited her to sit down. His eyes, when they met hers, were also filled with warmth.

"Are you okay?" she said, in reference to Matthew's death.

"Yes." His answer was appreciative.

Toby settled himself quickly on the floor at a distance from them. Rupert offered to play a game with him, but the boy declined.

"Talk to Thenie ... she's going way," he said with an innocent smile.

Athena looked again at her brother with an eyebrow cocked.

Rupert smiled, but Athena felt heavy-hearted at the mention of her departure.

"How many days?" he said.

"Three."

There was a silence. Rupert coughed.

"How's your research progressing?"

Athena made exaggerated nods of her head before speaking. She felt like she was choking.

"Good ... Good."

Oh God, she thought to herself, pull yourself together.

"You're not mad, I've decided," she said with a small laugh.

Rupert laughed aloud.

"I'm happy, and relieved, to accept your verdict, but I wouldn't discuss it with too many colleagues in Pennsylvania. They might not accept your findings."

Athena smiled at the joke, but again, her spirits lowered.

Rupert seemed to sense this and spoke more seriously.

"Are you finding it rewarding?"

She considered before answering. Did she? It seemed to Athena, that much had happened since she first interviewed Rupert. She remembered how avidly she had discussed her ideas with him, how confident and excited she was that her research, and that being done overseas, would lead to an understanding of the role of the brain and its chemistry in the formation of consciousness. She still believed this, and certainly the work she was doing was making a considerable contribution, but she was not so convinced that it mattered as much to her anymore.

Athena became alarmed at this thought. She had never allowed herself to admit it until now.

"I believe the work is worthwhile," she said, as much to herself as in answer to Rupert's question. "Any understanding of the brain has got to help ... to ... overcome prejudice towards mental conditions, for example."

"And in your particular area?" The question was asked with genuine interest, although Athena had to avoid Rupert's gaze, otherwise she became self-conscious.

"In my area?" she repeated, as a way of buying time to think. "It's important to know who we are, and how it is that we experience moments of awe ... and love." She felt herself blush as she said it and promised herself not to slip up again.

"And why?"

Athena didn't understand Rupert's question.

He explained. "You said it's important to know *how* it is that we experience those moments. Will we ever know why?" Rupert did not seem to be expecting an answer from her, his question trailing off while he seemed to ponder a new thought. He was not facing her now and, Athena thought, he looked terribly sad. He continued, as if to the floor, "When there is a conflict between these emotions, awe, and I assume you mean mystical awe, and love, are we in a position to make a choice?"

Once again, Athena did not think he required an answer. She couldn't answer it anyway, she decided, except that she knew which way she would choose.

Looking at him, in casual clothes and in this house, she was reminded of the Rupert she had seen dressed for the Mass. Rupert the Priest.

"I saw you the other day," she said tentatively, not knowing where she was going with this admission.

His eyebrows lifted in surprise.

She continued, "In the College Chapel. You were saying the Mass."

Rupert's eyebrows shot up further. He was smiling but looked perplexed.

"I was curious, I suppose."

Athena didn't need to explain any further. She could tell by Rupert's changed expression that he knew why. He looked apologetic.

There was an awkward pause. Athena realized that she had hoped for something in return for her admission, a denial, a rational explanation for the way he was that day. But his expression did not provide her with what she needed, and she felt, in that moment, like a jilted lover. She was embarrassed and bewildered as to why she would have thought that he felt for her, as she knew she felt for him. She wanted to go, but the telephone rang. Rupert blew through his teeth and seemed reluctant to leave her, but the telephone persisted.

"I'm so sorry," he said heading to the kitchen, "please stay; we need to talk."

When he had left, Athena sank back into the couch and closed her eyes. Pennsylvania may not come soon enough.

With a sigh, Rupert picked up the receiver, and was met with Kat at the other end.

"Have you heard from Neti, Ru?"

There was a hysterical tone to her voice that made him concerned.

"No, what's wrong?"

"She's gone ..."

When prompted by Rupert, Kat admitted that Neti had not been seen for two days.

"What did the police say?" he could feel his voice becoming tight with fear.

"I haven't called them yet." Kat mumbled it, and Rupert could hear the familiar tone of warning in her voice.

"Why?" he demanded.

"I thought she'd come back."

"For God's sake." He let out a long, exasperated sigh that held its own warning.

Rupert ran through possibilities with Kat. Was there a friend she had met? Did she leave a note explaining her absence?

Kat discounted these but mentioned the money that had been taken from her purse.

Rupert sighed. It was a considerable sum and, more significantly, he knew that it was not within Neti's character to take it unless she was desperate. It was too much to have to come back to explain. Rupert knew then that Neti had run away.

"Kat," he said in what was to be heard as a command, "ring the police, now. I'll contact the Melbourne police, and *please ring me* if you hear *anything!*"

Kat's voice was plaintive as she agreed.

Rupert wasted no time reporting Neti's disappearance. To his frustration, the policewoman at the other end of the telephone seemed to be not the least concerned.

"This happens all the time," she half-heartedly tried to reassure him, "she'll come back when she's hungry."

"No," he said firmly, "Neti doesn't do this all the time."

He returned to the lounge room. Athena and Toby were playing a game on the floor, and for a moment, his heart lurched at the sight. Immediately, Athena sensed that something was wrong, and Rupert told her about Neti, taking comfort in Athena's good sense and support.

"Where do you think she could be, Rupert?"

"I have an idea, that she's coming home, but I don't know if that's wishful thinking. It's a long trip for a fifteen-year-old on her own ..." He couldn't bear to think through the possibilities.

"Train? Or bus? Or ..." Athena's voice trailed off, but Rupert knew that she was going to say, hitchhiking. Although Neti could be impulsive, Rupert had faith that she had more sense than that. He'd heard Ross speak to her, several times, about potential dangers.

"My guess is train. It's faster, though more expensive, but she took enough money from Kat to be able to buy a ticket, I dare say."

Rupert was still standing in the middle of the room, not sure what his next move might be. He didn't know whether to wait for the police to call, or Kat. Athena decided for him.

"You sit down for a moment," she said with authority. "I'm going to ring the Rail people to find out the times of possible trains." She didn't wait for an answer, much less an argument, and headed to the kitchen. When she glanced back, Toby was cuddling into Rupert on the couch.

Toby looked up into Rupert's face. "Be all right," he said soothingly.

Rupert smiled and placed his arm around the young boy while he considered what he should do.

When Athena came back in, she looked hopeful. "7:30 tonight. The train from Byron Bay."

Rupert let out a constrained sigh. He looked at his watch; 6:45.

"You go, Rupert," Athena said. "Toby and I'll stay here, if you like, in case there's a call."

"Yeah," Toby wholeheartedly agreed.

Rupert was grateful for her offer and her concern and winced at the thought of what had transpired between them before Kat's call. She'd been embarrassed telling him that she'd gone to the Chapel; he had been moved but had been unable to tell her that. She was going away, he had to get used to the idea.

Gently, he prised himself free of Toby's clasp and collected his keys.

"Thank you, Athena," he said standing close to her. "You're ... a good friend."

A flicker of something he couldn't read, swept across her face.

"A pleasure Rupert ... from one friend to another. Take care."

Neti's sleep had come in fits and starts. There were thirty-six people in her carriage; she had counted them several times for something to do. Thankfully, no one had sat next to her. During the daylight hours, their noise had brought her some comfort, but, during the night, the relative silence made her uneasy and the vulnerability she felt prevented her from sleeping. In those dark hours too, her thoughts seemed to increase in their intensity and bleakness.

When Neti had left Kat, though she didn't have a plan, the morning light had given her courage, and she was sure that it would all work out, if she could only get home. But questions, in the night depleted that courage and she was uncertain now what her future would hold. Why was there an answering machine installed on the telephone at home? she wondered. Would Rupert welcome her back? She had left him without a word of goodbye; perhaps he was angry and would say "You made your bed ..." as she'd heard people say. In her heart, though, Neti doubted that. Was her uncle still at the house, or had he left it to return to the College? She couldn't blame him, nor could she expect him to give it up for her again. How would she manage if no one would look after her? The thought caused her such anxiety that Neti fell forward to ease the cramp of tension she was feeling in her abdomen. Perhaps Polly and her family would take her in? but Neti felt no comfort in this thought. She had often thought that her best friend was so lucky, to have a normal home, father, mother, brats for brothers and sisters. Life seemed to be so ordinary, the greatest stresses coming from a batch of burnt cupcakes or the constant teasing of Penny's brother, Jack. But Neti knew that this was not *her* family. And when she thought of life with her father, and then with Rupert, she felt that her own life had been just fine. How she wanted it back.

Neti thought of Athena and felt a small rise of optimism. Perhaps she'd help somehow, or, if nothing else, she could talk to her.

The seat was hard and unyielding to her body and her mouth tasted sour from the chocolate bar and sleep. Outside, the light was waning, and street and house lights told her that she was approaching Melbourne. Although the carriage was air-conditioned, Neti could feel the cooler Victorian air finding its way to her bones. It comforted her. In the twilight, the suburbs looked grey and gloomy, but it was where she wanted to belong. This was *her* city, her home. She wanted it to take her back and feared that she would have to travel from one place to another to live. She thought again of her room in its lamplight, the imaginary friends of her youth locked into the cornices and ornate ceiling, her collections of rocks and, she thought with pain and some private embarrassment, her worn and scraggly teddy bear lying under her bed.

The train slowed. There was a quiet hum of voices and the odd cracking of bones as people stretched and began collecting luggage from overhead lockers. Neti felt that she should look busy, but her bag had remained in her lap for the entire trip.

She had seen other people put their luggage overhead, but she hadn't wanted to stand up and draw attention to herself.

As the train lurched into Southern Cross Station, Neti felt her stomach lurch with it, sensing that what happened from here would be a defining moment in her life.

But she didn't know what to do.

Neti stepped from the carriage tentatively. It was quite dark now, and the other passengers were jostling past her to greet loved ones, or just to make a hasty departure. She wished that she could do either, to look at least like she knew what to do.

And then she saw him. A dark figure standing quietly, but she could tell his outline, like her father's, and even from a distance she saw that he was anxious. He always was.

And Neti ran, blindly, wildly knocking disembarking passengers on the way, and fell, sobbing, toward her uncle.

She was home.

Little was said on the way home, the emotion of their reunion still lingering and too important to be broken up by too many words. There would be plenty of time, Rupert thought. He looked over at his niece, who was leaning toward the passenger door, not in avoidance of him; she seemed to be snuggling the seat, her smile peaceful.

Neti was tired, he could see that clearly, but otherwise she looked well. Her hair seemed to have outgrown its spikes and lay more smoothly around her face, making her look older. There was a change to her expression that he couldn't quite determine: a subtleness perhaps.

Rupert thought of how fearful he had been that she would

not be on the train, and the overwhelming relief he felt when
he saw her running through the crowd. That moment, when
she embraced him, was his defining moment. A new life.

Athena was waiting at the door when the car pulled into
the drive. Toby stood at her side. They greeted them home with
such excitement that Rupert felt it was truly a celebration.
Toby grabbed Neti's hand and led her to the games on the floor.

"Not now, Tobe," Athena said apologetically to Neti, but
Neti did not seem the least bothered and joined Toby with
genuine pleasure. "We'll get going soon," she said to Rupert.

He smiled at her, a broad smile that he couldn't contain. He
was so utterly relieved.

"Please stay a while," he said, "Toby's got other ideas
anyway."

A sobering thought crossed his mind.

"I need to ring Kat, and the police. Will you excuse me?"

Athena nodded and joined the two on the floor.

In the kitchen, Rupert wished that he could avoid speaking
to Kat, but knew that he must. This time, though, he knew
where Neti wanted to be, and that made all the difference.
Despite his frustrations with Kat, he did feel some pity for her.
He suspected that she really did want to be a good mother, but
just didn't know where to begin. She had left it ten years too
late.

"I want to speak to Neti," she said, not willing to believe
Rupert, but he was adamant that she would have to wait until
Neti was ready. He would encourage her to ring, Rupert
assured her, and meant it.

Predictably, Kat laid the blame on Ross, on Guy, but never
on herself. Rupert didn't believe her. He knew her too well and
knew that she suffered for her neglect. He just hoped that she
did not repeat her mistake. By the end of the conversation, she

seemed to be resigned to Neti's decision, and hung up with a note of closure.

When he put down the receiver, Rupert felt as if the greatest load had been removed from his shoulders. He stepped into the lounge room with a lighter gait.

They were unaware of him standing there, and Rupert observed them quietly for a moment. He thought of the community members at Matthew's funeral, and what had held them together — that intangible quality; it was here too. He thought of the voice on the cliff that night in his youth, and how loudly and certainly he had heard it. Life had become crowded and complex, and his uncertainties had silenced that voice. But he knew what he was witnessing at this moment, these significant people in his life, who had renewed his sense of meaning.

He thought that he heard a whisper; it wasn't in his head, it was in his heart. Matthew had known; he had touched him there that day in the garden.

Where is your heart, Elijah?

End

Dear reader,

We hope you enjoyed reading *Whispers In The Wiring*. Please take a moment to leave a review, even if it's a short one. Your opinion is important to us.

Discover more books by Amanda Apthorpe at https://www.nextchapter.pub/authors/amanda-apthorpe

Want to know when one of our books is free or discounted? Join the newsletter at http://eepurl.com/bqqB3H

Best regards,

Amanda Apthorpe and the Next Chapter Team

You might also like:
A Single Breath by Amanda Apthorpe

To read the first chapter for free, please head to:
https://www.nextchapter.pub/books/a-single-breath

ACKNOWLEDGMENTS

The creation of this novel has never been a solo project, and I thank the following people in particular for their support: Miika Hannila of Next Chapter, Helen Goltz of Atlas Productions, Robin Grove, Peter Steele SJ, Joan Ryan, Olga Lorenzo, my friends, my family and, above all, my partner, Chris.

ABOUT AMANDA APTHORPE PHD

Amanda loves to write. No sooner has she inserted the final full stop on the latest novel and she's already shaping up for the next one. Amanda also loves to teach and to share with her students what she knows, and what she's still learning about writing. She holds a Master of Arts, and PhD in Creative Writing and is active in the national and international writing worlds, presenting at conferences and writing workshops.

Whispers in the Wiring is Amanda's first novel, but it is now accompanied by: *A Single Breath, Hibernia* and *One Core Belief.* In addition to writing fiction, Amanda has two published volumes of the *Write This Way* series: 'Time Management for Writers' and 'Finding Your Writer's Voice.'

Amanda is a Melbourne (Australia) based author, teacher and life-long student of yoga.

Whispers In The Wiring
ISBN: 978-4-86751-052-0

Published by
Next Chapter
1-60-20 Minami-Otsuka
170-0005 Toshima-Ku, Tokyo
+818035793528

26th June 2021

CPSIA information can be obtained
at www.ICGtesting.com
Printed in the USA
LVHW030135130721
692461LV00003B/294

9 784867 510520